Collins

U0108739

初階英語語法及寫作
GRAMMAR RULES

商務印書館

Acknowledgements

We would like to thank the following organizations for permission to reproduce photographs: sxc.hu – Martina, Bev Lloyd-Roberts, Miguel Saavedra, Hvaldezl, Odan Jaeger, Aneta Blaszczyk

Originally published in English by HarperCollins Publishers Ltd. under the title:
Collins Grammar Rules
© 1997 Angus Rose   Richard Purkis
Collins Grammar Rules (Second Edition)
© 2013 Angus Rose   Richard Purkis
Adaptation and Translation © 2004 The Commercial Press (Hong Kong) Ltd.
Adapted and translated under licence from HarperCollins Publishers Ltd.

Collins 初階英語語法及寫作
Collins Grammar Rules

作　　者：Angus Rose　Richard Purkis
翻　　譯：香港教育圖書有限公司編輯部
責任編輯：黃家麗
封面設計：趙穎珊
出　　版：商務印書館 (香港) 有限公司
　　　　　香港筲箕灣耀興道 3 號東滙廣場 8 樓
　　　　　http://www.commercialpress.com.hk
發　　行：香港聯合書刊物流有限公司
　　　　　香港新界大埔汀麗路 36 號
　　　　　中華商務印刷大廈 3 字樓
印　　刷：美雅印刷製本有限公司
　　　　　九龍觀塘榮業街 6 號海濱工業大廈 4 樓 A
版　　次：2020 年 6 月第 1 版第 1 次印刷
　　　　　©2020 商務印書館 (香港) 有限公司
　　　　　ISBN 978 962 07 0576 2
　　　　　Printed in Hong Kong

目錄

1 詞彙 The Word

2 詞組與句子
Word Groups and the Sentence

3 進階寫作技巧
Advanced Writing Skills

1 詞彙 The Word

A 詞類 Parts of speech

B 造詞 Word building

C 拼寫指南 Spelling guide

D 使用字典 Using a dictionary

E 同義詞與反義詞 Synonyms and antonyms

詞類 Parts of speech

英語詞彙可分成八個類別，統稱為「詞類」（'parts of speech'）：

- nouns 名詞
- pronouns 代詞
- verbs 動詞
- adjectives 形容詞

- adverbs 副詞
- prepositions 介詞 / 介系詞 / 前置詞
- conjunctions 連詞 / 連接詞
- interjections 感歎句

每種詞類在句子中擔當不同工作。

'We thought we'd call him Noun.'

「我想我們會叫他<u>名詞</u>。」

名詞（nouns）替事物取名。

名詞 Nouns

名詞（nouns）一般解作名稱，用引號括住。名詞可包括人、地、物件、羣組、質素及觀點的名稱。名詞共分為四類：

- proper 專有
- common 普通
- collective 集體
- abstract 抽象

專有名詞 Proper nouns

名詞（proper nouns）是指某一人、某組人、某地或某物的名稱，例如：

Elvis Presley（貓王皮禮士利）　　*the Beatles*（披頭四）
Queen Victoria（維多利亞女皇）　　*London*（倫敦）
Ramadan（齋月）　　*Boeing 747*（波音 747）
Africa（非洲）

注意！

所有專有名詞皆以大楷字母開首：

Mickey Mouse and *Roger Rabbit* went to *Disneyland Paris* and met *Goofy* at *Camp Davy Crockett*.

米奇老鼠和羅傑兔到了法國迪士尼樂園，他們在克德維營遇見高飛。

普通名詞 Common nouns

專有名詞以其專有名稱來單指某一事物，但普通名詞（common noun）則指一些有共同特徵的物件或動物：

dog（狗）　*flower*（花）　*car*（車）　*road*（道路）　*bacon*（煙肉）

普通名詞不以大楷字母開首（除非是作為一個句子之首）。

A head chef is a person who goes into a kitchen and orders the staff.

主廚是指一個走進廚房指點員工的人。

集體名詞 Collective nouns

集體名詞（collective noun）即一羣人或一組事物的名稱：

band（樂隊），即 *a group of musicians*（一班樂手）；*herd*（獸羣），即 *a group of cows*（一羣牛）；*team*（隊伍），即 *a group of sports players*（一羣運動員）；*crew*（組或隊），即 *a group of sailors*（一隊水手）；*audience*（觀眾）、*congregation*（會眾）、*pack*（羣或隊）、*gang* 幫或夥）

集體名詞（collective nouns）可作單數（singular）或複數（plural）使用——只要你認為哪個較合適便可：

單數：The band is playing at 9 o'clock.
　　　樂隊會於 9 點演奏。

複數：The band are going back to their homes for tea.
　　　樂隊成員會各自回家吃下午茶。

切忌混合使用單數和複數，如：

✗ The class left their seats before it was told to.
　　那班學生在獲得許可前離開了坐位。

✔ The class left their seats before they were told to.

抽象名詞 Abstract nouns

抽象名詞（abstract noun）是指那些我們在思想上可理解，但卻不能用五官（five senses）來感受的東西。換言之，抽象名詞並非我們所能看見、聽見、觸摸、品嚐或嗅到的東西，例如：

excitement（興奮）	*courage*（勇氣）
happiness（快樂）	*fear*（恐懼）
misery（悽慘）	*anger*（憤怒）
hope（希望）	*possibility*（可能性）

抽象名詞不以大階字母開首（除非是作為一個句子之首）。

> **More to Learn**
>
> 某些名詞可視乎其用法而屬於多於一個名詞組別：
>
> *a pride of lions* 一羣獅子（集體名詞）
> *full of pride* 滿懷自信（抽象名詞）

辨別名詞：怎樣辨認名詞
Noun spotting: how to recognize a noun

你可用以下方法辨認一個句子中的名詞。

• 以下詞彙常緊置於名詞之前：

a	an	the	some
any	my	his	her
their	this	that	those

a ball（一個球）	*the tractor*（該拖拉機）
any news（任何新聞或消息）	*my goodness*（我的天）
her house（她的房子）	

- 某些名詞有特定詞尾：

  -*tion*: ***station*** (車站)   ***action*** (行動)   ***description*** (描述)

  -*ness*: **happi*ness*** (快樂)   **empti*ness*** (空虛)   **thick*ness*** (厚度)

  -*ism*:   **magnet*ism*** (磁力學)   **terror*ism*** (恐怖主義)

  -*or*:   **doct*or*** (醫生)   **act*or*** (演員)   **sail*or*** (水手)

  -*ing*:   **swimm*ing*** (游泳)   **eat*ing*** (進食)   **talk*ing*** (説話)

EXTRA Information 你可在「感歎句 Interjections」的
「辨別詞類──用疑問方法」中找到更多竅門。

名詞特徵 Features of a noun

名詞有三個主要特徵：

- 可數 (countability) 或不可數 (non-countability)
- 性別 (gender)
- 詞格 (case)

名詞有可數的或不可數的。可數名詞可以是單數或複數的：

car   cars (車)   *orange   oranges* (橙)

不可數的名詞只有單數，並無複數：

happiness (快樂)   *beef* (牛肉)   *humour* (幽默)   *sunlight* (陽光)

More to Learn

某些名詞看似是複數，但其實是單數：

news（新聞）　　*measles*（痲疹）

physics（物理）　*home economics*（家政）

然而，某些名詞只有複數，並無單數：

scissors（剪刀）　*glasses*（眼鏡）

trousers（褲子）　*thanks*（感謝）

名詞也有性別。名詞的性別有四類：

- 男性（masculine）：

  man（男人）　*boy*（男孩）　*bull*（公牛）　*sailor*（水手）

- 女性（feminine）：

  woman（女人）　*girl*（女孩）　*cow*（母牛）　*actress*（女演員）

- 中性（neuter），即非男性或女性：

  music（音樂）　　*bucket*（圓桶）　　　*coffee*（咖啡）

  tent（帳幕）　　*gymnastics*（體操）

- 共用（common），即男性或女性：

  child（小孩）　*person*（人）　*athlete*（運動員）

名詞有詞格。在英語中主要有三種詞格：

- 主語詞格（subject case）或規範詞格（nominative case）：

  The <u>pencil</u> broke. 鉛筆斷了。

- 賓語格（object case）或賓格（accusative case）：

  Read the <u>notice</u>. 請閱讀告示。

• 屬有格 (possessive case) 或領屬格 (genitive case)：

The team's kit 隊伍的裝備

Sara's hat 莎拉的帽

EXTRA Information 見第二章「詞序 Word Order」。

複數名詞 Plural nouns

表示複數名詞的常見方法是加上 -s：

pen–pens (筆) *house–houses* (房屋) *train–trains* (火車)

但在許多情況下，以上規則並不適用：

• 以 -ch、-s、-sh、-ss 或 -x 結尾的名詞會加上 -es 以示複數，(否則我們便無法讀出複數名詞)：

pitch–pitches (足球場) *bus–buses* (巴士)

gash–gashes (傷口) *mattress–mattresses* (床墊) *fox–foxes* (狐狸)

• 對於以輔音 (consonant) + -y 結尾的名詞，須改 -y 為 -ies 以表示複數：

baby–babies (嬰兒) *pastry–pastries* (酥皮批) *party–parties* (派對)

然而，對於以元音 (vowel) + -y 結尾的名詞，則可如常加上 -s 以表示複數：*donkey–donkeys* (驢子) *valley–valleys* (山谷) *Monday–Mondays* (星期一)

• 改以 -f 或 -fe 結尾的名詞為以 -ves 結尾，來表示複數：

loaf–loaves (麵包) *half–halves* (一半) *wife–wives* (妻子)

但這規則亦非永遠可行：

roof–roofs (屋頂) *chief–chiefs* (領袖) *safe–safes* (保險箱)

- 大部份以 -o 結尾的名詞都加上 -es 以表示複數：
  *hero–hero**es*** (英雄)
  *tomato–tomato**es*** (番茄)
  *potato–potato**es*** (馬鈴薯)

- 某些名詞的單數和複數是相同的：
  one sheep (一隻綿羊)　*two sheep* (兩隻綿羊)
  one deer (一隻鹿)　　*two deer* (兩隻鹿)
  one trout (一條鱒魚)　*two trout* (兩條鱒魚)

注意！

千萬別加撇號 (apostrophe') 來表示複數。許多人也犯了這個錯誤呢！

代詞 Pronouns

代詞 (pronouns) 是用來代替名詞 (nouns) 的詞彙。代詞可造成以下句子：

Mrs Jones told <u>her</u> son Ron to take <u>his</u> bike out of <u>her</u> car.

鍾斯太太叫兒子朗從她的車裏拿他的腳踏車出來。

用來代替如下例般的累贅句子：

Mrs Jones told <u>Mrs Jones's</u> son Ron to take <u>Ron's</u> bike out of <u>Mrs Jones's</u> car.

鍾斯太太叫鍾斯太太的兒子朗從鍾斯太太的車裏拿朗的腳踏車出來。

代詞分類 Types of pronouns

代詞有七類，分為：

- 人稱（personal）
- 物主（pooooooivo）
- 反身（reflexive）
- 指示（demonstrative）

- 疑問（interrogative）
- 關係（rolativo）
- 不定（indefinite）

人稱代詞 Personal pronouns

人稱代詞（personal pronouns）用於人和物：

I（我）	me（我）	you（你）	he（他）
she（她）	it（它）	we（我們）	us（我們）
you（你們）	they（他們）	them（他們）	

物主代詞 Possessive pronouns

物主代詞（possessive pronouns）表明某人或某物屬於誰人或何物：

mine（我的）　yours（你的）　hers（她的）　ours（我們的）　theirs（他們的）

注意！

Yours（你的）、hers（她的）、ours（我們的）和 theirs（他們的）等物主代詞從不加上撇號（apostrophe'）。

反身代詞 Reflexive pronouns

反身代詞（reflexive pronouns）呼應其主語（subject）：

myself（我自己）　　　yourself（你自己）　　himself（他自己）
herself（她自己）　　　itself（它自己或牠自己）　ourselves（我們自己）
yourselves（你們自己）　themselves（他們自己）

I will do the job myself.
我會親自辦理。

She saw herself on the TV.
她在電視上看見自己。

You left yourselves with no choice.
你們沒為自己留下任何選擇。

They hid themselves.
他們藏起自己。

指示代詞 Demonstrative pronouns

指示代詞（demonstrative pronouns）能指示名詞或代詞，例如：

this（這）　　　　these（這些）　　　them（他們）
such（這或那）　　one（一個 [代詞]）　ones（一些 [代詞]）
none（無 [代詞]）

This is the train for Beijing.
這列是往北京的火車。

These are the keys.
這些是鑰匙。

Your bike is smaller than that.
你的腳踏車比那輛還要小。

Such is the case.

就是這樣。

疑問代詞 Interrogative pronouns

疑問代詞（interrogative pronouns）提出疑問：

who（誰）？   which（哪人或物）？
what（甚麼）？   whose（誰人的）？

Who paid?

誰付錢？

Which have you bought?

你買了哪個？

What did you say?

你説甚麼？

Whose glasses are these?

這副眼鏡是誰的？

關係代詞 Relative pronouns

關係代詞（relative pronouns）能連繫已提及的人或物，例如：

who（用於指人，包括主語和賓語）   which（用於指物，包括主語和賓語）
whom（用於指人，只限賓語）   whose（用於指某人或物的）
that（用於指某物；偶爾使用）

The admiral, who by now had turned green, often gets seasick.

那個面色已變青的艦隊司令時常暈船。

The car which I drive is an old banger.

我駕駛的車是一輛破舊汽車。

The girl <u>whom</u> I mentioned is here.

我曾提及的女孩在這裏。

The lady <u>whose</u> keys we needed was out.

保管我們所需鑰匙的女子不在家。

The house <u>that</u> Jack built

傑克興建的房屋

不定代詞 Indefinite pronouns

不定代詞 (indefinite pronouns) 泛指人或物，其數量並無明確界定，例如：

anyone (任何人或有人)   someone (有人)   several (幾個)

some (一些)   none (無)   sometimes (有時)

one (某一)   they (他們或人們)

Can <u>anyone</u> hear me?

有人聽到我說話嗎？

<u>Someone</u> belched. Who was it?

有人打嗝，是誰？

The noise upset <u>several</u> people. <u>Some</u> reacted angrily.

噪音滋擾了幾個人，有些人表示憤怒。

<u>None</u> of them were deafened.

他們無一聽不見。

<u>One</u> must not make rude noises.

人不可發出不禮貌的噪音。

<u>They</u> say the house is haunted.

人們說這屋鬧鬼。

代詞的三種人稱 The three persons of pronouns

人稱代詞（personal pronouns）可以是單數（singular）或複數（plural），
各有三種人稱：

- 第一人稱單數（指説話者或作者）：I（我）
- 第二人稱單數（指説話者的對象）：you（你）
- 第三人稱單數（指説話者在談及的人或物）：he（他）、she（她）、it（它或牠）
- 第一人稱複數：we（我們）
- 第二人稱複數：you（你們）
- 第三人稱複數：they（他們）

人稱 Personal

	人稱 (person)	主語 (subject)	賓語 (object)	物主* (possessive)	反身 (reflexive)
單數 (singular)	1	I（我）	me（我）	mine（我的）	myself （我自己）
	2	you（你）	you（你）	yours（你的）	yourself （你自己）
	3	he（他）、 she（她）、 it（它或牠）	him（他）、 her（她）、 it（它或牠）	his（他的）、 hers（她的）、 its（它的或 牠的）	himself （他自己）、 herself （她自己）、 itself （它自己或 牠自己）
複數 (plural)	1	we （我們）	us （我們）	ours （我們的）	ourselves （我們自己）
	2	you （你們）	you （你們）	yours （你們的）	yourselves （你們自己）
	3	they （他們、她們、 它們、牠們）	them （他們、她們、 它們、牠們）	theirs （它們的或 牠們的）	themselves （它們自己或 牠們自己）

***EXTRA** Information* 見第一章「物主形容詞」。

關係代詞 Relative pronouns

性別（gender）	主語（subject）	實語（object）	物主（possessive）
男性（masculine）或 女性（feminine）	who （用於指人）	whom （用於指人）	whose （用於指某人的）
中性（neuter）	which （用於指物）	which （用於指物）	whose （用於指某物的）

指示代詞　Demonstrative pronouns

	單數（singular）	複數（plural）
near（近處）	this（這）	these（這些）
far away（遠處）	that（那）	those（那些）

動詞 Verbs

'Looks like I'm going to VERB you!'
「看來我會『動詞』你啦！」

動詞（verbs）說明動作。

動詞（verbs）是最重要的詞彙，是每個句子必要有的。
動詞說明的東西有二：

- 名詞（noun），或代詞（pronoun）的動作：

  The door opened. 門打開了。

  The milkman entered. 送牛奶的人走進來。

  I thought he was going to cry. 我以為他會哭。

- 名詞（noun），或代詞（pronoun）的狀態：

  He is so upset. 他現在很失落。

  His van wheels are wobbly. 他的貨車車輪正搖晃不定。

  He will be in trouble. 他將有難。

動詞的主要類別 Main types of verbs

動詞主要分三類：

- 及物（transitive）
- 不及物（intransitive）
- 助動（auxiliary）

及物動詞 Transitive verbs

及物動詞（transitive verb）後接賓語（object）。

EXTRA Information 見第二章「詞序 Word Order」。

換言之，及物動詞所表達的動作會影響到某人或某物。

主語（subject）	動詞（verb）	賓語（object）
Richard	*helped*	*the old lady*
李察	幫助	那位老太太。
The striker	*kicked*	*the ball.*
那前鋒	踢	那球。

不及物動詞 Intransitive verbs

不及物動詞（intransitive verb）之後沒有賓語（object）。例如，你不能説「顫抖（shiver）某人」或「打噴嚏（sneeze）某人」。

主語（subject）	動詞（verb）	沒有賓語（no object）
My granny	*shivered.*	—
我的外婆	顫抖。	—
The princess	*sneezed.*	—
公主	打噴嚏。	—

More to Learn

某些動詞（verbs）可以是及物動詞或不及物動詞，用法視乎上文下理而定：

及物（transitive）	不及物（intransitive）
She rang the bell.	*The bell rang.*
她按響鈴鐘。	鈴鐘響起來。
I opened the door.	*The door opened.*
我開門。	門開了。

助動詞 Auxiliary verbs

助動詞即「幫助」分詞（participle）或不定式（infinitive）的動詞（verbs）。
要造出完整的動詞，見注意事項。（auxiliary 是幫助的意思。）

最常見的助動詞有 be、have、must、may、can、do。

It <u>is</u> raining. 正下着雨。

I <u>have</u> opened my umbrella. 我已打開
了雨傘。

Bilal <u>ought</u> to open hers.
拜娜應打開她的雨傘。

The rain <u>may</u> stop soon.
雨可能快要停下來了。

We <u>could</u> have sheltered.
我們本可避雨的。

It <u>does</u> look like it's stopping.
雨似真快要停了。

動詞中最重要的兩部份
Two important parts of the verb

不定式　The infinitive

這是動詞的原形（base form），通常前接 'to'
使用：

to fly（飛翔）　　*to waste*（浪費）
to swim（游泳）　*to ache*（疼痛）

分詞　The participle

任何動詞也有兩種分詞（participles），分別是現在分詞（present
participle）和過去分詞（past participle）。

現在分詞（present participle）常以 -ing 結尾：

bathing（洗澡）　　*walking*（步行）
writing（寫作）　　*doing*（做／進行）

過去分詞（past participle）常以 -ed 結尾：

parted（分開）　*dusted*（抹塵）　*rubbed*（磨擦）　*prepared*（準備）

三種主要時態 Three main tenses

動詞的時態（tense）表明動作何時進行（或將何時進行，又或已於何時進行）。

主要時態有三種：

- 現在（present）
- 過去（past）
- 將來（future）

現在式　Present tense

現在式（present tense）用於表示現在進行的動作：

I sing 我是唱歌的　　　　　　　*I am singing* 我正在唱歌
I do sing 我確實是唱歌的

過去式　Past tense

過去式（past tense）用於表示已過去的動作：

I sang 我以前是唱歌的　　　　　*I was singing* 我當時在唱歌
I did sing 我以前確實是唱歌的　　*I had sung* 我從前曾唱歌

將來式　Future tense

將來式（future tense）用於表示將要進行的動作：

I shall sing 我將會唱歌　　　　　*I am going to sing* 我打算唱歌
I am about to sing 我準備唱歌　　　*I shall be singing* 屆時我會在唱着歌

規則（regular）或「弱」（'weak'）動詞的表現形式如下：

現在式 （present tense）	過去式 （past tense）	過去分詞 （past participle）	將來式 （future tense）
I watch 我看	*I watched* 我看了	*[I have] watched* ［我曾］看過	*I shall watch* 我將會看
He plays 他玩耍	*He played* 他停止了玩耍	*[He has] played* ［他曾］玩耍	*He will play* 他將會玩耍
They use 他們使用	*They used* 他們使用了	*[They have] used* ［他們曾］使用	*They will use* 他們將會使用

不規則（irregular）或「強」（'strong'）動詞的過去式不會在詞尾加上 -ed，而是改變拼寫方法。（所有優質的字典也有列出其變化。）

現在式 （present tense）	過去式 （past tense）	過去分詞 （past participle）	將來式 （future tense）
I sing 我是唱歌的	*I sang* 我以前是唱歌的	*[I have] sung* ［我曾］唱歌	*I shall sing* 我將會唱歌
He deals 他處理（某事）	*He dealt* 他以前處理（某事）	*[He has] dealt* ［他曾］處理（某事）	*He will deal* 他將處理（某事）
We think 我們認為	*We thought* 我們從前認為	*[We have] thought* ［我們曾］認為	*We shall think* 我們會認為
They eat 他們吃	*They ate* 他們吃完了	*[They have] eaten* ［他們曾］吃過	*They will eat* 他們將會吃
Tom goes 湯姆往（某地）	*Tom went* 湯姆從前往（某地）	*[Tom has] gone* ［湯姆已］往（某地）去	*Tom will go* 湯姆將往（某地）

More to Learn

一致金律！   King Concord!

ⓧ The girls <u>am</u> going into town.
女孩們打算往市鎮去。

ⓧ Dave <u>are</u> a good footballer.
德菲是一位出色的足球員。

以上例子當然是錯誤的！根據一致規則（concord rule），動詞（verb）與主語（subject）的人稱（person）和數量（number）之間的關係必須一致。如主語是第一人稱單數（first singular），其動詞必須是第一人稱單數；如主語是第二人稱複數（second plural），其動詞必須是第二人稱複數……如此類推。

在虛擬的情況下，這規例是可以打破的：

✔ If I <u>were</u> king...
如果我是皇帝的話……

其他時態 ： 完成式及進行式
Other tenses: the perfect and the continuous

除三種主要時態外，還有兩種時態是我們需要學習的：

• 完成式（perfect）

• 進行式（continuous）

動作完成和結束時應使用完成式：

I *have eaten*. 我已經吃過了。

You *have been warned*. 你已遭警告了。

過去分詞（past participle）常用來構成完成式（perfect tenses）：

eaten（吃）   *warned*（警告）

若動作已進行了一段時間，縱使動作可能從前已開始，其時態卻是進行式（continuous）：

Charlie is laughing.
查理在笑。

I have been waiting here for an hour.
我在此已等候了一個小時（現在我仍在等候）。

Charlene had already been camping.
莎蓮已在露營。

現在分詞（present participle），即 -ing 形式，可用來構成進行式（continuous tenses）：

More to Learn

分詞（participles）可作動名詞（verbal nouns），例如：

Swimming is great exercise.
游泳是有益身心的運動。

Many people enjoy dancing.
很多人都愛跳舞。

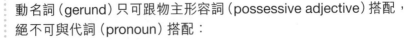

The dying and the dead lay on the battlefield.
戰場上滿佈垂死的人和死屍。

（在英語中，動名詞名為 gerunds。）

動名詞（gerund）只可跟物主形容詞（possessive adjective）搭配，絕不可與代詞（pronoun）搭配：

I was sorry about his going.（不是 *'him going'*）
我對他的離去感到難過。

Your saying that reminds me...（不是 *'you saying'*）
你那番提醒我的説話……

此外，分詞（participles）也可用作動形容詞（verbal adjectives），如：

a swimming pool 一個泳池

a talking canary 一隻會説話的金絲雀

a sunken wreck 一艘沉沒了的破船

a clapped-out old banger 一輛破爛不堪的舊汽車

（在英語中，動形容詞名為 'gerundives'。）

語態 Voices

動詞（verb）的「語態」（'voice'）指出動作是由主語（subject）所做，或是由某人或某物對主語所做的。

語態有兩種：
・主動（active）
・被動（passive）

主動語態　Active voice

動作由主語（subject）所做：

We read the play aloud. 我們放聲朗讀劇本。

The sun shines. 太陽照耀。

People breathe. 人們呼吸。

They are speaking. 他們正在說話。

You have helped him. 你曾幫助他。

被動語態　Passive voice

動作由某人或某物對主語（subject）做的（雖然句子未必指出動作由何人或何物所做）：

The play was read aloud by the cast.
劇本由演員們放聲朗讀。

Diana was let down (by her friend).
戴安娜（對朋友）感到失望。

It has been decided (by the committee).
決定已（由委員會）作出了。

形容詞 Adjectives

'Well... it's a very... ADJECTIVE painting.'
「好……這真是一幅很『形容詞』的畫。」

形容詞（adjectives）描述事物。

形容詞（adjectives）是為名詞（nouns）或代詞（pronouns）提供更多資料的詞彙。形容詞常緊置於所描述之詞彙前：

a lively game show 一個生動的遊戲節目

big prizes 豐富的獎品

Lucky you! 幸運的你！

形容詞的類別 Types of adjectives

形容詞（adjective）主要有六類：

- 描述（descriptive）
- 指示（demonstrative）

- 物主（possessive）
- 疑問（interrogative）
- 數字（numerical）
- 數量（quantitative）

描述形容詞　Descriptive adjectives

描述形容詞（descriptive adjectives）描述事物。這類形容詞是最常見的：

wonderful world　奇妙的世界

happy people　快樂的人

wild animals　野生動物

指示形容詞　Demonstrative adjectives

指示形容詞（demonstrative adjectives）指明事物：

this rain　這場雨

those bends　那些彎路

such crazy driving　如此瘋狂的駕駛技倆

EXTRA Information　可同時參考第一章「注意」內有關「冠詞」的內容。

物主形容詞　Possessive adjectives

物主形容詞（possessive adjectives）指出物件屬於何人或何物：

my fingers　我的手指

your door　你的門

their parrot　他們的鸚鵡

its beak　牠的嘴

領屬格（possessive）'its'（解作「牠的或它的」時）是不用加上撇號（apostrophe [']）的：

The dog lost its bone. 那頭狗失去了牠的骨頭。

疑問形容詞　Interrogative adjectives

疑問形容詞（interrogative adjectives）用於發問：

Which house? 哪間屋？　*Whose car?* 誰的車？

數字形容詞　Numerical adjectives

數字形容詞（numerical adjectives）指出：

- 數字（number）：

  seven birds 七隻鳥

  one hundred dancers 一百位舞蹈員

  each pupil 每位學生

- 事物的次序（the order of things）：

  first team 第一隊

  second thoughts 三思

  final whistle 最後通牒

- 不定數字（indefinite number）：

  several problems 幾個問題

  some ideas 一些念頭

  few answers 很少答案

數量形容詞　Quantitative adjectives

數量形容詞（quantitative adjectives）指出事物的數量：

a <u>little</u> bit of curry 一點咖喱

<u>more</u> ice cream 多些冰淇淋

a <u>whole</u> bar of chocolate 一整塊巧克力

<u>much</u> pain 劇痛

注意！

冠詞
The articles

冠詞（the articles）the、a 和 an 全是指示形容詞（demonstrative adjectives）。

the 是定冠詞（definite article）。

a 或 an 是不定冠詞（indefinite article）。

an 用於以元音（vowel）開首的名詞（noun）：

an apple 一個蘋果

an orange 一個橙

an idiot 一個笨蛋

辨別形容詞：怎樣辨認形容詞
Adjective spotting: how to recognize an adjective

提示一

形容詞（adjectives）常緊置於所形容的名詞（noun）之前：

an <u>enjoyable</u> book 一本引人入勝的書

或透過動詞（verb）與名詞（noun）連上：

Motorways are <u>noisy</u>. 高速公路是很嘈吵的。

提示二

你可從形容詞的詞尾（後綴 [suffix]）來辨認。最常見的有：

後綴	例子
-able 或 -ible	*probable*（可能的）、*terrible*（可怕的）、*likeable*（討人喜歡的）
-al	*general*（一般的）、*actual*（實際的）、*vital*（重要的）
-ary	*military*（軍事的）、*stationary*（靜止的）
-en	*broken*（破爛的）、*fallen*（淪陷的）、*sunken*（沉沒的）
-ful	*useful*（有用的）、*awful*（糟透的）、*dreadful*（討厭的）
-ic	*poetic*（有詩意的）、*terrific*（極好的）、*artistic*（藝術的）
-ish	*childish*（幼稚的）、*selfish*（自私的）、*brownish*（帶棕色的）
-ive	*active*（活躍的）、*persuasive*（令人信服的）、*massive*（巨大的）
-less	*hopeless*（絕望的）、*brainless*（愚蠢的）、*homeless*（無家可歸的）
-ous	*serious*（嚴重的）、*marvellous*（絕妙的）、*famous*（著名的）
-some	*troublesome*（麻煩的）、*handsome*（貌美的）、*loathsome*（令人厭惡的）
-y	*tricky*（詭計多端的）、*bumpy*（崎嶇不平的）、*rubbery*（似橡膠的）

形容詞的比較 Comparison of adjectives

形容詞（adjectives）有三種比較程度：
- 原級（positive）
- 比較級（comparative）
- 最高級（superlative）

原級　Positive

這是形容詞最基本的形式：

happy（快樂的）　*old*（年老的）　*honest*（誠實的）

比較級　Comparative

比較級指出名詞（noun）有更多原級（positive）的素質（quality）：

happier（更快樂的）　*older*（更年老的）　*more honest*（更誠實的）

最高級　Superlative

最高級指出名詞（noun）原級屬性（positive quality）所能具備的最高程度：

happiest（最快樂的）　*oldest*（最年老的）　*most honest*（最誠實的）

比較級（comparative）和最高級（superlative）常以加上 -er 和 -est 來表示：

cold（冷）　*cold**er***（更冷）　*cold**est***（最冷）

然而，以上規則並非永遠可行的：

- 若形容詞以輔音（consonant）+ y 結尾，則刪去 y，然後加上 -ier 或 -iest：

  messy（凌亂的）　*mess**ier***（更凌亂的）　*mess**iest***（最凌亂的）
  dry（乾涸的）　*dr**ier***（更乾涸的）　*dr**iest***（最乾涸的）

- 若遇上字母較多的形容詞，或當加上 -er 和 -est 後讀起來會感到奇怪時，就用 more 和 most：

honest（誠實的） *more honest*（更誠實的） *most honest*（最誠實的）
horrible（可怕的） *more horrible*（更可怕的） *most horrible*（最可怕的）
complimentary（讚美的） *more complimentary*（更讚美的）
most complimentary（最讚美的）

有些形容詞有不規則比較級（irregular comparative）和最高級（superlative）：

原級 （positive）	比較級 （comparative）	最高級 （superlative）
good（好）	*better*（更好）	*best*（最好）
many（多）	*more*（更多）	*most*（最多）
little（少）	*less*（更少）	*least*（最少）

注意！

比較兩件事物時，運用比較級（comparative）：

Dan is quite tall; but Harry is <u>taller</u>.
丹是挺高大的；但哈利更高大。

Manchester City was the <u>better</u> of the two teams.
曼徹斯特城是兩隊之中較優秀的。

比較三件或以上的事物時，運用最高級（superlative）：

This is the <u>best</u> answer of all.
這是所有答案之中最好的。

This was the <u>worst</u> thing that could happen.
這是最糟糕的事。

副詞 Adverbs

Gloria glides ADVERBIALLY on the ice.
歌莉亞在冰上「副詞地」滑翔。

副詞（adverbs）為動詞（verbs）提供更多資料。

副詞（adverbs）會提供更多有關動詞（verbs），或有時關於形容詞（adjectives）的資料。副詞常放在最近動詞的位置，以及在其他詞類（parts of speech）之前：

He drove dangerously. 他危險駕駛。

Sirius is a very bright star.
天狼星是一顆非常明亮的星星。

She spoke almost inaudibly.
她說話低聲得幾乎聽不見。

副詞種類 Types of adverbs

副詞有七類：

- 方式（manner）
- 地點（place）
- 時間（time）
- 原因（reason）
- 次數（number）
- 程度（degree）
- 否定（negation）

方式副詞　Adverbs of manner

回答 'How（怎樣）?' 的疑問：

Marge spoke <u>slowly</u>. 瑪芝慢慢地說。

The rescuers worked <u>furiously</u>. 救援人員奮力搶救。

地點副詞　Adverbs of place

回答 'Where（哪裏）?' 的疑問：

Towser barked to go <u>outside</u>. 豆斯吠着要出去。

Please stand <u>there</u>. 請站在那邊。

時間副詞　Adverbs of time

回答 'When（何時）?' 的疑問：

I hope she arrives <u>soon</u>. 我希望她快些來到。

Few girls are called Gertie <u>nowadays</u>.
現在很少女孩名叫積蒂了。

原因副詞　Adverbs of reason

回答 'Why（為甚麼）?' 的疑問：

They were <u>therefore</u> promoted.
他們因此而獲升職。

The meeting was cancelled <u>because of</u> the storm.
會議因風暴而取消了。

次數副詞　Adverbs of number

回答 'How many（多少）?' 的疑問：

He did it <u>once</u>, but not <u>again</u>.
他做過一次，但不再做了。

程度副詞　Adverbs of degree

回答 'How much（多麼）?' 或 'To what degree or extent（何等程度或地步）?' 的疑問：

The bull was <u>very</u> annoyed.
那頭公牛很不耐煩。

Mrs Jones was <u>extremely</u> upset too.
鍾斯太太也極難過。

否定副詞　Adverbs of negation

'not'（「不」）是副詞，有時 'neither... nor'（「既不……也不」）也是副詞：

She would <u>not</u> laugh.
她不會笑。

He <u>neither</u> sang <u>nor</u> whistled.
他既不唱歌，也不吹口哨。

More to Learn

副詞也可……   Adverbs can also...

…… 與形容詞、其他副詞、短語，甚至整個句子連用。

與其他副詞連用 ： With other adverbs:

He spoke __painfully__ slowly.
他說話緩慢得令人難受。

The rider fell __quite__ heavily. 騎師摔得甚為嚴重。

與短語連用 ： With phrases:

The film about Humpty Dumpty was __completely__ off the wall.
那齣關於雞蛋先生的電影極之怪誕。

The driver was not __entirely__ in the wrong.
錯不全在於那位司機。

與整個句子連用 ： With whole sentences:

__Sensibly__, Mrs Jones didn't annoy the bull any further.
鍾斯太太識趣不再惹怒那頭公牛。

Pigs __definitely__ are not able to fly.
豬肯定不會飛。

辨別副詞：怎樣辨認副詞
Adverb spotting: how to recognize an adverb

提示一

大部份的副詞（adverb）皆以 -ly 結尾。要使形容詞（adjective）變成副詞，加上 -ly 是常見方法：

形容詞	副詞
quick（快速）	*quickly*（快速地）
usual（慣常）	*usually**（慣常地）

* 留意 *usually*（慣常地）中有兩個 '*l*'。

More to Learn

- 以 -ly 結尾的不一定是副詞（adverb）！例如：

  fly（飛行）　　*lovely*（可愛的）　　*bully*（惡霸）

  holy（神聖的）　*ugly*（醜陋的）

- 某些副詞有其特有形式：

  soon（快要）　　*now*（現在）　　*here*（在這裏）　　*also*（同樣）

- 某些副詞跟其形容詞（adjectives）是相同的：

  fast（快）　　*long*（長）　　*early*（早）

  close（接近）　*near*（在近處）

  形容詞：*a fast car* 一輛快車
  副詞：*she drove fast* 她開車很快
  形容詞：*the early bird* 早起的鳥
  副詞：*they arrived early* 他們早了到埗

提示二

若有需要的話，以短語 'in a ... way' 來代替副詞（adverb）。這可避免使形容詞如 'lovely'（「可愛的」）轉變成駭人而且不存在的副詞如 'lovelily'。説 'in a lovely way' 較為容易可行。

副詞的比較 Comparison of adverbs

副詞（如形容詞般）有三種比較程度：

- 原級（positive）
- 比較級（comparative）
- 最高級（superlative）

原級　Positive

這是副詞（adverb）最基本的形式，正如以上所提及的：

soon（快要）　*slowly*（緩慢地）　*smoothly*（順利地）

比較級　Comparative

比較級指出動詞（verb）或形容詞（adjective）有更多原級（positive）的素質（quality）：

sooner（更快地）　*more slowly*（更慢地）　*more smoothly*（更順利地）

最高級　Superlative

最高級（superlative）意謂動詞或形容詞的原級屬性所能具備的最高程度：

soonest（最快）　*most slowly*（最慢）　*most smoothly*（最順利）

表示比較級（comparative）和最高級（superlative）的常則有：

- 如副詞（adverb）只有一個音節，加上 -er 和 -est：

soon（快）　　*soon**er***（更快）　　*soon**est***（最快）
near（近）　　*near**er***（更近）　　*near**est***（最近）

- 如副詞（adverb）多於一個音節，在前面加上 more（更）和 most（最）：

smoothly（順利地）、***more** smoothly*（更順利地）、***most** smoothly*（最順利地）；*sincerely*（誠懇地）、***more** sincerely*（更誠懇地）、***most** sincerely*（最誠懇地）。

注意！

當你比較兩種情況時，切記用比較級：

David eats <u>more greedily</u> than a hippopotamus.
大衛比一隻河馬還要貪吃。

用最高級來比較三種或以上的情況、人物等等：

Of all the staff, Mr Chan teaches <u>most enthusiastically</u>.
在所有職員之中，陳先生最熱衷於教學。

Grammar Clinic

別在副詞（adverb）的位置使用形容詞（adjective）。

以下是錯誤的例子：

✗ *He writes much <u>neater</u>.*

以下是正確的例子：

✓ *He writes much <u>more neatly</u>.*
　他寫字更整齊。

以下是錯誤的例子：

✗ *Why doesn't she speak <u>proper</u>?*

以下是正確的例子：

✓ *Why doesn't she speak <u>properly</u>?*
　為甚麼她說話不得體？

介詞 Prepositions

介詞（prepositions）連起名詞（noun）。

介詞（prepositions）是連起兩個名詞（或代詞）的詞彙。

The train went <u>through</u> the tunnel. 火車駛過隧道。

在以上句子中，'through' 展示如何連起 'train'（「火車」）和 'tunnel'（「隧道」）。

The girl was the daughter <u>of</u> a film star.
那女子是某電影明星的女兒。

在上例中，'of' 連起 'girl'（「女子」）和 'film star'（「電影明星」）。

介詞必須放在兩個相連結的名詞（或代詞）之間，並緊置於第二個名詞之前：

He dropped the banana <u>from</u> the window.
他從窗戶丟下香蕉。

It fell <u>in front of</u> the bulldozer.
它跌落在推土機前。

介詞包括：

about（關於）	above（在……之上）	across（經過）
after（之後）	against（與……相反）	along（隨着）
amid（在……當中）	around（環繞）	at（在）
before（之前）	behind（後面）	below（在……之下）
beneath（在……之下）	beside（在旁邊）	
between（在……之間）	beyond（在……之後）	by（在旁邊）
down（向下）	except（除了）	for（為了）
from（從）	in（在內）	inside（在裏面）
like（相似）	near（接近）	of（……的）
off（離開）	over（越過）	since（自從）
through（穿過）	till（直到）	to（向着）
towards（朝着）	under（在……之下）	until（直到）
up（朝上）	upon（在）	with（與）

複合介詞（Compound prepositions）由多於一個字組合而成：

apart from（除了） because of（因為） due to（由於） in front of（在……前面）

More to Learn

有很多詞彙可同時用作介詞（preposition）和副詞（adverb）：

介詞：*He put a belt <u>round</u> his sagging trousers.*
　　　他用一條皮帶束着寬鬆的褲子。

副詞：*She turned <u>round</u> to face him.* 她轉身面向他。

辨別兩者最有效的方法是：

介詞（*preposition*）必定後接名詞（*noun*）、代詞（*pronoun*）或類似的短語（*phrase*）。在以上第一個例子中，由於 '*round*' 後接 '*his sagging trousers*'（「寬鬆的褲子」），故 '*round*' 必是介詞。

連接詞 Conjunctions

連接詞（conjunction）連結句子的不同部份。

連接詞（conjunctions）連結句子不同部份的詞彙。

主要的連接詞有：

and（和）	because（因為）	but（但是）
for（為）	however（然而）	since（自從）
until（直至）	yet（但是）	

連接詞的種類 Types of conjunctions

連接詞（conjunctions）有四類：

- 並列（co-ordinating）
- 對比（contrasting）
- 相關（co-relative）
- 從屬（subordinating）

並列連接詞　Co-ordinating conjunction

若相連的物件是類似的，可運用並列連接詞（co-ordinating conjunction），如 and（和）、as（也一樣）和 moreover（而且）：

Both Butch and Tiddles like fish very much.

畢和泰德兩人都很喜歡魚。

Butch likes fish, as does Tiddles.
畢喜歡魚，泰德也一樣。

對比連接詞　Contrasting conjunction

若相連的物件各不相同，則運用對比連接詞（contrasting conjunction），如 but（但是）、however（然而）、yet（但是）：

I can't even ride a bike, but my granny is an astronaut.
我連怎樣騎腳踏車也不懂，但我的祖母卻是一位太空人。

相關連接詞　Co-relative conjunction

要強調相連的物件是類似的，就運用相關連接詞（co-relative conjunctions），例如 'both + and'（「兩者……都」）；'either + or'（「不是……就是」）；'so + as'（「像……那麼」）；'not only + but also'（「不但……而且」）：

Grandpa wore not only a crash hat but also lycra shorts.
祖父不但戴上防護帽子，而且還穿上了彈性短褲。

從屬連接詞　Subordinating conjunction

若相連的物件有着主從關係，可以運用從屬連接詞（subordinating conjunction），例如：

after（之後）	because（因為）	for（為）	since（自從）
till（直至）	when（當）	although（雖然）	

As I walked out onto the stage, I was really nervous.
當我走上舞台時，我感到非常緊張。

Although she could play hockey well, she preferred to watch.
雖然她精於玩曲棍球，但是她寧願當觀眾。

在以上例子中，'I was really nervous' 是句中的主句（main clause）。若沒有這主句，則分句（clause）'As I walked out onto the stage' 也就無法理解了。

EXTRA Information 見第二章的「主句」和「從句」。

Grammar Clinic

雖然連接詞（conjunctions）用於連結事物，但有
時也會用於句首：

While in Paris, I went up the Eiffel Tower.
當我在巴黎時，我走上艾菲爾鐵塔。

As Mummy was ill, I cooked lunch.
因為媽媽病倒了，所以由我弄午餐。

More to Learn

- 在英語中，連接詞（conjunctions）和介詞（prepositions）有時稱作連詞（connectives）。
  （如果你不明白原因，可參看第一章「介詞」和「連接詞」。）

- 'and'（「和」）和 'but'（「但」）只會在強調某點時才放在句首：
  He lost his car. He lost his licence. And he lost his temper.
  他失去了他的車。他失去了車牌。他還大發脾氣。

感歎句 Interjections

> 感歎句（interjections）可單獨使用，並不含語法功能。

感歎句（interjections）一般是單獨使用的詞彙，常用來表達強烈的感情：

oh（噢）！　　　　*phew*（啊）！　　　　*drat*（討厭）！
yippee（妙極）！　*hurrah*（好啊）！　　*hello*（喂）！

這些詞彙沒有語法功能，而且差不多在句中的任何位置也可出現。

A：*My grandad lived to be 104.*
　　我祖父活到 104 歲。

B：*Really?*
　　真的？

A：*Yes, after 70 he never changed his socks.*
　　真的，他 70 歲之後便不再換襪子了。

B：*Blimey!*
　　不是吧！

A：*His feet didn't half smell especially, yuk, at meal times.*
　　吃飯的時候他的腳尤其臭得厲害。

B：*Eargghhh!!!!*
　　真嘔心！

辨別詞類—用疑問方法
Spotting parts of speech — the question method

'Looks like the NOUNS have landed.'
「看來『名詞』已經着陸了。」

要辨別名詞，可提問在動詞之前是 'What'（甚麼）？'、'Who'（誰人，作主語用）？' 或 'Whom（誰人，作賓語用）？'。

若要知道句中的各種詞類（parts of speech），可試用以下建議：

名詞和代詞 Nouns and pronouns

要辨認名詞（noun）和代詞（pronoun），可提問 'What（甚麼）？'、'Who（誰人，作主語用）？' 或 'Whom（誰人，作賓語用）？'：

The elephant charged through the undergrowth.
大象衝過灌木叢。

What charged（甚麼動物衝）？
──→ elephant（大象）：名詞

Through what（衝過甚麼）？

──→ undergrowth（灌木叢）：名詞

She asked me about our holiday.
她問我有關我們度假的事。

Who asked（誰問）？
──→ she（她）：代詞

Whom did she ask（她問誰）？
──→ me（我）：代詞

What about（關於甚麼）？
──→ holiday（度假）：名詞

動詞 Verbs

要辨認動詞（verbs），可提問 'What does [or did] the subject do（主語做 [或做過]甚麼）？'：

She asked me if I was OK.
她問我有沒有大礙。

What did she do（她做了甚麼）？
──→ asked（問）：動詞

但是，要辨認在被動語態（passive voice）中的動詞，（見第一章詞彙），就要問 'What was done to the subject（主語遇上甚麼事）？'：

My ankle was broken by the tackle.
我的腳踝給滑輪弄碎了。

What was done to the ankle（腳踝遇上甚麼事）？
──→ was broken（給弄碎了）：動詞

提示

不及物（intransitive）的「狀態」動詞（'being' verbs）在未學懂之前是甚難辨認出來的，包括 to be（am, are, is, were 等）、to appear（似乎）、to seem（看來）。

The house is green. 房子是綠色的。

She seems lonely. 她看似寂寞。

They appear normal. 他們看似正常。

形容詞 Adjectives

要辨認形容詞（adjective），可提問 'Which（哪些）？'、'What kind of（怎麼樣的）？' 或 'How many（多少）？'：

Those boys are working hard.
那班男孩非常努力。

Which boys（哪些男孩）？
────→ those（那些）：形容詞

The green apples stayed on the branches.
青蘋果留在樹枝上。

What kind of apples（怎麼樣的蘋果）？
────→ green（青色的）：形容詞

Three men entered the old house.
三個男人走進舊屋裏。

How many men（多少男人）？
────→ three（三個）：形容詞

What kind of house（怎麼樣的屋子）？
────→ old（古舊的）：形容詞

副詞 Adverbs

- 要辨認副詞（adverb），可提問 'How（怎樣）？'、'Where（哪裏）？'、'When（何時）？' 或 'Why（為甚麼）？'：

Yesterday Mr Grotch's Rolls Royce rolled smoothly downhill, ending up in the river.

昨天高先生的勞斯萊斯順暢地向山下滑行，最後落到河裏去。

How did it roll（車滑行得怎樣）？

────➤ smoothly（順暢地）：副詞

Where did it roll（它在哪裏滑行）？

────➤ downhill（向山下）：副詞

When did it roll（它何時滑行）？

────➤ yesterday（昨天）：副詞

- 但若要辨認與動詞（verbs）連用的程度副詞（adverbs of degree），可問 'How much（多麼）?' 或 'To what extent（何等程度）?'：

Mr Grotch was very annoyed.

高先生非常煩惱。

How much was Mr Grotch annoyed（高先生有多煩惱）？

────➤ very（非常）：副詞

- 要辨認與形容詞（adjectives）和副詞（adverbs）連用的程度副詞（adverbs of degree），可提問 'How（多麼）?'：

Her extremely old grandfather walked very slowly.

她那位極年老的祖父走路非常慢。

How old（年紀有多大）？

────➤ extremely（極為）：副詞

How slowly（有多慢）？

────➤ very（非常）：副詞

More to Learn

not(「不」)永遠也是副詞(adverb)。

介詞 Prepositions

如果要辨認介詞(preposition),可在句中找出多個名詞(noun)或代詞(pronoun),然後查看它們是否連結在一起。接著,找出連結它們的詞彙。

The box remained under the table. 箱子留在桌子下面。

'box'(「箱子」)和 'table'(「桌子」)是名詞(noun);'under'(「在⋯⋯下面」)指示出箱子與桌子在位置上的關聯,因此證明 'under' 是介詞。

介詞(通常)必要後接名詞或代詞。

(在拉丁文中,'pre' 是「在前面」的意思,故 'preposition' 這名字指在名詞或代詞前面的位置。)

溫習 Revision

A. 圈出正確答案來完成文章。

(1.'What's / Which's) happened?' (2. Me / My) mum asked me when she heard me crying.

(3. 'Anybody / Somebody) stole my bike!' (4. I / my) said. I was so upset, but luckily, my friend knew someone who was selling (5. their / they) bike so I bought (6. those / that) one. The lady (7. whose / whom) bike it was before took extremely good care of it. I bought it for a very decent price too so I was pleased with (8. herself / myself)! (9. She / Her) was very kind.

B. 圈出正確答案來完成句子。

1. Her mother was (most extreme / extremely) upset when she heard the news.

2. He really wanted to buy (a / some) clothes, but he had no money.

3. He ran up the steep hill very (slowly / slow).

4. There were two huge (fish / fishes) in the tank.

5. The (wolfes / wolves) howled in the night.

6. He was so (anger / angry) with me.

7. She was afraid of (the / some) dark.

8. 'When is she arriving?' 'She's arriving (soon / sooner).'

9. 'I hate (that / those) vegetables,' she said.

10. I would love to eat a juicy (orange / oranges) right now.

11. There was not enough room on the (buses / bus) for everyone.

12. He needed to buy (an / a) avocado, but he couldn't find one anywhere.

13. There were hundreds of (mosquitoes / mosquitos) in the jungle.

14. There was (any / a) possibility that he would fail the exam.

15. 'Why was the netball match cancelled?' '(Because of / Therefore) the storm.'

C. 圈出正確動詞。如不需要動詞，請用「x」標示。

Yesterday I (1. took / take) my Mum out for lunch. She (2. is / was) fired from her job last week so I wanted to cheer her up. We (3. went / shall go) to a lovely restaurant and ate some delicious food.

Today I am meeting my friend. We were (4. go / going) to have a picnic in the park but it (5. x / is) raining, so we (6. are / were) going swimming instead. Swimming is such good exercise so I want to start (7. done / doing) it more. I must (8. finished / finish) my homework first though and revise for my exams. I haven't even (9. started / starting) my revision yet!

D. 以下方框包含形容詞（如 **several**、**long** 等）及名詞（如 **puppy**、**people** 等）。用其中一個形容詞及一個名詞來完成句子。

> adorable   bag   book   difficult   exam   holiday   interesting
> large   long   people   puppy   several   strong   wind

1. I am very relaxed because I have just been on a _____ .

2. She had a _____ because she had so much to carry.

3. The _____ whistled through the house.

4. His _____ is only six weeks old!

5. There were _____ at the football match.

6. I read a really _____ yesterday.

7. He failed the _____ .

My short hair is black and spiky.

E. 用下列方框內的介詞（如 under、at 等）或連接詞（如 and、so 等）來完成文章。

> after and as behind but from
> up over so under with while

Last weekend, my friend 1. _____ I went to an outdoors adventure centre. The obstacle course was very challenging. We had to crawl 2. _____ nets, jump 3. _____ streams and climb 4. _____ trees. I was exhausted 5. _____ all of this, 6. _____ that wasn't the end, we still had paintballing to do! We were both really tired, 7. _____ we decided to rest for a few minutes before paintballing.

We were in a team with two other boys who were both lovely. I found a huge tree to hide 8. _____ so I didn't get hit very much! 9. _____ I enjoyed paintballing, I don't think I'll do it again 10. _____ it was quite sore. I spent most of my time running away 11. _____ people!

F. 圈出正確答案。如不需要加入文字，請用「x」標示。

(1. Me / My) mum and I (2. went / go) shopping yesterday to buy new clothes. (3. She / Her) didn't buy anything, but I bought a (4. little / few) dresses, a pair of trousers and (5. a / x) winter jacket. Hurray (6. me / x) ! The jacket is so (7. beauty / beautiful). It's long, woolen (8. but / and) colourful. After shopping, we went to a restaurant which is very famous for its

pasta. We watched the (9. amazingly / amazing) talented chefs make the spaghetti right in front of us. It made me want to make my own pasta (10. at / in) home but I know that mine won't be as good as (11. them / theirs.)

G. 將以下句子改為疑問句,使句子中粗黑的文字變為答案。第一題為範例。

Sentence	Question
1. **The boy** broke his arm.	Who broke his arm?
2. Frank is going to **France** today.	
3. She shouted at **James**.	
4. **It was raining** so they had to go inside.	
5. **Ten** people came to the show.	
6. She bought a **beautiful dress**.	
7. The man ran **quickly**.	
8. He is arriving **tomorrow**.	

造詞 Word building

詞綴（前綴和後綴）Affixes (Prefixes and Suffixes)

'Not THAT sort of root!'
「不是指*那*種根！」

詞根（root）是詞彙的基本部份。

詞根（root）意指基本詞彙，藉着它可造成其他詞彙（word）。例如，詞根 'cover'（「隱藏」）可變成 uncover（揭露）、discover（發現）、recover（復原）、covering（遮蓋物）、rediscovery（重新發現）等等。

詞彙中新的零碎部份 un-、dis-、-ing 等稱為「詞綴（affixes）」。詞綴有兩個種類：

- 前綴（prefixes）
- 後綴（suffixes）

前綴（prefix）是一組有特定意思的字母，放在詞根（root）的前面：

tele - vision（電視）、*anti* - septic（消毒劑）、*geo* - graphy（地理）

後綴（suffix）是一組有特定功能的字母，放在詞根（root）的後面：

good - *ness*（善良）、million - *aire*（百萬富翁）、disturb - *ance*（騷亂）

辨別形容詞：怎樣辨認形容詞
Adjective spotting: how to recognize an adjective

造詞可用以下方法：

- 前綴（prefix）+ 詞根（root）

  semi + circle（半圓形）

- 詞根（root）+ 後綴（suffix）

  laugh + able（可笑的）

- 甚至是前綴（prefix）+ 詞根（root）+ 後綴（suffix）

  under + stand + ing（理解）

  re + cover + able（可復原的）

前綴及其意思 Prefixes and their meaning

盡量多學前綴（prefix）的意思，可以幫助你明白大量生詞的意思。

前綴為數甚多，以下只是常見的一小部份：

前綴	意思	例子
pre	*before*（之前）	*pre*-cook（預先煮好）
anti	*against*（對抗）	*anti*-aircraft（防敵機的）
mis	*wrong*（錯誤）	*mis*understand（誤會）
multi	*many*（許多）	*multi*coloured（多色的）
post	*after*（之後）	*post*script（後話）
semi	*half*（一半）	*semi*circle（半圓形）
con、co	*with*（與）	*con*tract（合約）
ex	*out of*（出）	*ex*port（出口）
ad	*to*（朝向）	*ad*mit（許可進入）

字典（dictionary）會單獨列前綴為中心詞（headwords）。遇上新前綴或新詞根時可翻查字典。

後綴及其意思 Suffixes and parts of speech

- 名詞（noun）後加上後綴（suffix）-ic 就變成形容詞（adjective）：

  名詞：*photograph*（相片）

  形容詞·*photographic*（攝製的）

  名詞：*scene*（風景）

  形容詞：*scenic*（風景優美的）

- 後綴 -or 造出名詞（noun），意謂「做某動作的人」：

  動詞：*sail*（海上航行）

  名詞：*sailor*（水手）

  動詞：*direct*（指導）

  名詞：*director*（導演）

  動詞：*conduct*（指揮）

  名詞：*conductor*（指揮家）

一些常見的後綴及其功用
Some common suffixes and what they do

- 製造名詞（nouns）：

後綴	例子
-er、-or	*buyer*（買家）、*tutor*（導師）
-ess	*actress*（女演員）、*princess*（公主）
-ism	*magnetism*（磁學）、*vandalism*（恣意破壞的行為）
-ment	*ornament*（飾物）、*pavement*（行人路）
-ness	*goodness*（善良）、*wickedness*（邪惡）
-ice	*advice*（忠告）、*practice*（練習）
-ship	*friendship*（友誼）、*kinship*（親屬關係）

- 製造動詞（verbs）：

後綴	例子
-en	*frighten*（嚇怕）、*strengthen*（加強）
-fy	*horrify*（驚嚇）、*magnify*（放大）

- 製造形容詞（adjectives）：

後綴	例子
-able	*lovable*（可愛的）、*drinkable*（可喝的）
-ful	*beautiful*（美麗的）、*useful*（有用的）
-less	*helpless*（無助的）、*harmless*（無害的）

- 製造副詞（adverb）：

後綴	例子
-ly	quickly（快捷地）、strangely（奇怪地）

今後你會遇上更多後綴。每當你遇上一個新後綴時，用筆記下，並找出它造成甚麼詞類。

派生詞 Derivatives

派生詞（derivatives）是指一個由加上前綴（prefix），有時再加上後綴（suffix），所造出來的新詞（new word）。試找出所有可從這表造出來的派生詞，如：

photo + graph + y = photography（攝影）。

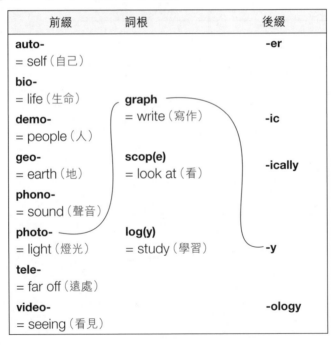

前綴	詞根	後綴
auto- = self（自己）		**-er**
bio- = life（生命）	**graph** = write（寫作）	
demo- = people（人）		**-ic**
geo- = earth（地）	**scop(e)** = look at（看）	**-ically**
phono- = sound（聲音）		
photo- = light（燈光）	**log(y)** = study（學習）	**-y**
tele- = far off（遠處）		
video- = seeing（看見）		**-ology**

複合詞 Compounds

Horseplay
喧鬧的娛樂

複合詞（compound）由詞彙（word）拼合而成。

由兩個或以上詞彙（word）組合而成的新詞彙稱為複合詞（compound）。
複合詞中的連字符號（hyphen）則可有可無。

有連字符號的字 ： With hyphens:

long-ago（很久以前的）   *long-haired*（長髮的）
long-winded（喋喋不休的）   *long-legged*（長腳的）

> **EXTRA** *Information* 見第二章「詞彙裏的標點符號」有關連字符號的字。

沒有連字符號的字 ： Without hyphens:

starfish（海星）   *starship*（太空船）
stardust（夢幻感覺）   *starboard*（飛行器的右舷）

More to Learn

複合詞（compound word）的意思常跟當中詞彙的原本意思不同：

hop（跳）+ scotch（蘇格蘭威士忌）
　= hopscotch（跳房子遊戲）

sou'（南）+ wester（向西）
　= sou'-wester（護頸防水帽）

horse（馬）+ play（娛樂）
　= horseplay（喧鬧的娛樂）

溫習 Revision

A. 在橫線上填上正確的前綴或後綴來完成句子。

1. He helped the old lady out of the (good _____) of his heart.

2. She had to get a lot of (treat _____) for her broken leg.

3. He forgot to bring money with him. He was an extremely (forget _____) person.

4. Now he was a (billion _____), he could afford anything.

5. He stormed off and started crying so his mum told him he was being very (child _____).

6. He didn't want to (_____ mit) that he was wrong.

7. The (_____ violence) project helps students who have been bullied at school.

8. He never understood how to use a (_____ colon) to punctuate a sentence.

9. There was an extremely (_____ tasteful) smell in the room, so everyone went outside.

10. The squashed cake looked very (_____ appealing).

B. 在橫線上填上正確的前綴或後綴來完成文章。

Jack saw a (1. _____ view) of the film and though it looked really good, so he decided to go and watch it. While he was (2. watch _____) the film, he ate a huge bucket of popcorn which made him feel extremely sick! The film was very (3. enjoy _____) and he especially liked the main character — a lonely school boy who was (4. mis _____) by his peers. They all (5. _____ liked) him because they thought he was rude, but in fact, he was just very shy.

C. 用線將下列後綴及其詞根連接起來。

Root		Suffix
1. Buy •		• A. able
2. Excite •		• B. er
3. Fix •		• C. less
4. Hope •		• D. ment

D. 用方框 **1** 及 **2** 其中一個字組成複合詞，填在橫線上。如有需要，請加上連字符號 **(hyphen)**。

> **1.**
> action   sports   ice
> basket   well   out

> **2.**
> ball   side   skating
> packed   mad   known

It was a sunny day, so Sarah decided to do something 1. _____.
She called her friend who was 2. _____ and they arranged
to play a game of 3. _____. They met at a 4. _____
sports centre close to Sarah's house and played together for about an
hour.

Afterwards, they went 5. _____ in the mall which was
lots of fun. In the evening they went to the cinema to watch an 6.
_____ film. All in all, they had an extremely enjoyable day.

I'm a hardworking boy.

拼寫指南 Spelling guide

三個加強拼寫能力的提示 Three hints for better spelling

1. 口齒不清造成差勁的拼寫能力。要改善拼寫能力，在腦海中也要咬字清晰。字典通常會教授正確的發音方法。

   EXTRA *Information*　見第一章有關「發音」。

注意！

以下三個詞彙常因發音錯誤而導致拼寫錯誤：

specific（特定的）　undoubtedly（毫無疑問）　pronunciation（發音）

---

2. 大部份拼寫方法奇異的詞彙都是來自其他語言的：

   'Suede'（發音為 swayed）意謂絨面皮，源自法文 'suéde'，即指這類衣物的原產地——瑞典。

   'Disciple' 意謂追隨者，源自拉丁文 'discipulus'，意指學習的人。

   優質的字典常會記載詞彙的來源。

3. 訓練自己「拍照」，記下一些有拼寫困難的詞彙，在腦海中組合它們成為一幅清晰的照片。還要勇於發明一些幫助自己記憶的方法，例如：

   Parallel（平行線）一詞中間有兩條平行線。

Enlightenment：啟蒙

勇於發明一些幫助自己記憶的方法。

注意！

別忘記在英語詞彙中，每條常規（rule）總有一些例外情況（exceptions）。常規和例外情況均須學懂。

十一條常規 Eleven general rules

1. 當單音節詞彙以元音（vowel）＋輔音（consonant）結尾（如 hop），加上後綴（suffix）時，就要重複輔音（consonant），即 ho**pp**ing（跳躍）。

shop   ⟶   *sho**pp**ing*   （購物）

strap   ⟶   *stra**pp**ed*   （綑綁）

bat   ⟶   *ba**tt**ed*   （擊球）

bag   ⟶   *ba**gg**y*   （寬鬆）

sad   ⟶   *sa**dd**en*   （悲哀）

試想想如果不重複輔音，這些詞彙的發音會變成怎樣。

不過，若後綴以輔音起首，以上規則便不適用：

sad   ⟶   *sadly*   （憂傷地）

2. 當詞彙多於一個音節，而重音（accent）落在結尾的音節時，就要重複最後的輔音：

refer   ⟶   *referring*   （提及）

fulfil   ⟶   *fulfilled*   （完成）

occur   ⟶   *occurring*   （發生）

3. 以多於一個音節（syllable）的詞彙來說，短元音（short vowel）常後接一對重複的輔音：

短元音	長元音
hopping（跳躍）	*hoping*（希望）
cattle（牛）	*cater*（迎合）
carry（攜帶）	*caring*（關心）
dinner（晚餐）	*dining*（進餐）

4. 以單一個 'l' 結尾的詞彙，加上後綴時就要重複 'l'：

travel（旅遊）⟶ *traveller*（旅客）

marvel（奇蹟）⟶ *marvellous*（不可思議的）

但這規則並不適用於美式的拼寫方法。

5. 若作結尾的 'y' 前接輔音，加上後綴時就要變作 'i'：

beauty（美麗） ⟶ *beautiful*（美麗的）

bury（埋葬） ⟶ *buried*（埋葬）

lovely（可愛的）⟶ *lovelier*（更可愛的）

EXTRA *Information*　見第一章有關「複數」。

不過，基於發音的原因，後綴‘-ing’會保留‘y’：

carry ⟶ *carried*，但 *carrying*（攜帶）

steady ⟶ *steadier*，但 *steadying*（穩固）

6. 若後綴以元音起首，輔音後的 ‘e’ 會刪去，但若後綴以輔音起首，輔音後的 ‘e’ 則會保留：

use ⟶ *using* （使用），但 *useful* （有用）

care ⟶ *caring* （關心），但 *careful* （小心）

注意！

此規則（rule）有許多例外情況（exceptions）：

likeable （討人喜愛的）

sizeable （相當大的）

ageing （變老）

singeing （燒焦）

canoeing （划獨木舟）

這些詞彙的後綴以元音起首，但輔音後的 ‘e’ 並沒有刪去。

---

7. 接於輔音 ‘c’ 和 ‘g’ 後的 ‘e’ 通常也會保留下來；跟後綴 -able 和 -ous 並用時也是一樣：

change （改變） ⟶ *changeable* （可改變的）

notice （留意） ⟶ *noticeable* （顯著的）

courage （勇氣） ⟶ *courageous* （勇敢的）

8. 若複合詞由前綴和以 'll' 結尾的後綴組成，只需保留一個 'l'：

well	+	*come*	=	*welcome*	（歡迎）
all	+	*ways*	=	*always*	（永遠）
care	+	*full*	=	*careful*	（小心）
peace	+	*full*	=	*peaceful*	（和平的）
skill	+	*full*	=	*skilful*	（熟練的）

但也有例外情況（exceptions）的：

| *full* | + | *ness* | = | *fullness* | （完整） |
| *still* | + | *ness* | = | *stillness* | （靜止） |

9. 放 'i' 在 'e' 之前，除非在 'c' 後面，並發音成 'ee'；或並非在 'c' 後面，又非發音成 'ee'：

- 並非在 'c' 後面，但發音成 'ee' 時：

  brief（簡略）　*mischief*（搗蛋）
  piece（塊）　　*field*（田地）　　*niece*（姪女）

- 在 'c' 後面，但發音成 'ee' 時：

  receive（收到）　　*deceive*（欺騙）
  conceited（驕傲的）　　*ceiling*（天花板）

- 並非在 'c' 後面，又非發音成 'ee' 時：

  foreign（外地的）　　*leisure*（閒暇）　　*height*（高度）

- 在 'c' 後面，並非發音成 'ee' 時：

  science（科學）

|||||||||||||||||||||||||||||||||||||||||||||||||||||||||| **注意！** ||||||||||||||||||||||||||||||||||||||||||||||||||

seize（抓緊）和 weird（怪誕）是此規則的例外情況（exceptions）。

10. 動詞以 'c' 加上 'k' 結尾，並後接以元音起首的後綴：

picnic（野餐）⟶ *picnicker*（野餐的人）

panic（恐慌）⟶ *panicking*（恐慌）

frolic（嬉戲）⟶ *frolicked*（嬉戲）

11. 以 'ie' 結尾的動詞若加上後綴 '-ing'，就會變成：

lie ⟶ *lying*（説謊）

die ⟶ *dying*（死亡）

tie ⟶ *tying*（繫上）

注意！

無論加上前綴（prefixes）或後綴（suffixes），也要記得帶整個詞綴（affix）入詞彙裏：

accidental + **ly**	= *accidentally*	（意外地）
real + *ly*	= *really*	（真的）
cool + *ly*	= *coolly*	（冷漠地）
over + *run*	= *overrun*	（超時）
il + *literate*	= *illiterate*	（文盲的）
un + *noticed*	= *unnoticed*	（不顯著的）
mean + *ness*	= *meanness*	（吝嗇）
book + *keeping*	= *bookkeeping*	（簿記）
dis + *satisfied*	= *dissatisfied*	（不滿）

每當學習新詞彙的拼寫方法時，也要用新詞彙造句，作為練習，這樣便可同時學懂詞彙的意思。

溫習 Revision

A. 用正確拼寫來完成句子。

1. Betty loved writing _____ (story).

2. The dog was _____ (lie) on the cold floor.

3. As soon as he got _____ (pay), he went shopping.

4. They collected lots of _____ (berry) and made some delicious jam.

5. There are many amazing _____ (city) around the world.

B. 圈出正確答案來完成句子。

1. They were finding it difficult to book (accomodation / accommodation) in Turkey.

2. He had a huge (arguement / argument) with his girlfriend.

3. He checked his (calendar / calander) and realised that he was fully booked for the whole month.

4. Mrs Smith's child was very (independant / independent).

5. There were at least 10 celebrities there, which was a rare (occurrence / occurrance).

6. Even though he had a lot of (experiance / experience), he didn't get the job.

C. 圈出正確答案來完成文章。

Amy and her mum went (1. shoping / shopping) at the weekend to buy some new shoes. She was (2. hoping / hopping) to buy some for under $200, but she couldn't find any. In the end, she bought two pairs for $500.

In the evening, they went for (3. dinner / diner) at an Italian restaurant where they had a very (4. disapointing / disappointing) pizza, followed by an (5. excellent / excelent) (6. dessert / desert).

They went home and sat in front of the television and watched a film. They both enjoyed (7. puting / putting) their feet up after a long day of shopping!

D. 圈出文章內 10 個含拼寫錯誤的詞語。

At the begining of term, she didn't enjoy her new school as it was very dificult to fit because there weren't many foriegn students. She was very jelous of her classmates because they all wore the same clothes and were the same hieght, and she just looked so different! She managed to get though the first term, and decided that from then on, she'd make more of an effort.

The second term was so much better for her and she felt very priveleged to be part of such an amazing school. She made some lovely friends and was very gratful to have found them as they made her life a lot more enjoyable. She even recieved an award for the most improved student of the year. What an achievment!

E. 圈出拼寫正確的詞語。

1. i) heavier	ii) heaveir
2. i) skiing	ii) skying
3. i) panicking	ii) panicing
4. i) really	ii) realy
5. i) weird	ii) wierd
6. i) peice	ii) piece
7. i) commitment	ii) comittment
8. i) achieve	ii) acheive

使用字典 Using a dictionary

字典（dictionary）是很有用的。

字典（dictionary）不只記載詞彙的拼寫方法和意思。

詞彙按字母的先後次序（alphabetical order）排列。

在一本優質字典裏，可找到：

- 中心詞（headword）
- 複數（plural）
- 詞類（part of speech）
- 定義（definition）
- 詞源（origin）
- 複合詞（compound）和派生詞（derivative）
- 形容詞和副詞的比較級（comparative）與最高級（superlative）
- 短語（phrase）和慣用語（idiom）

成年人使用的字典還提供發音方法（pronunciation）。

north-westerly
1 (adjective) North-westerly means to or towards the north-west.
2 A north-westerly wind blows from the north-west.

north-western
(adjective) in or from the north-west.

Norwegian, Norwegians (pronounced nor-**wee**-jn)
1 (adjective) belonging or relating to Norway.
2 (noun) A Norwegian is someone who comes from Norway.
3 Norwegian is the main language spoken in Norway.

nose, noses, nosing, nosed
1 (noun) Your nose is the part of your face above your mouth which you use for smelling and breathing.
2 The nose of a car or plane is the front part of it.
3 (phrase) If you **pay through the nose** for something, you pay a very high price for it.
4 If someone **turns their nose up at** something, they reject it because they think it is not good enough for them.
5 (verb; an informal use) If someone noses into something, they try and find out about it when it is none of their business.

nosedive, nosedives
(noun) A nosedive is a sudden downward plunge by an aircraft.

nostalgia (pronounced nos-**tal**-ja)
(noun) Nostalgia is a feeling of affection for the past, and sadness that things have changed.
nostalgic (adjective), **nostalgically** (adverb).

nostril, nostrils
(noun) Your nostrils are the two openings in your nose which you breathe through.
[from Old English *nosu* meaning 'nose' and *thyrel* meaning 'hole']

nosy, nosier, nosiest; also spelled **nosey**
(adjective) trying to find out about things that do not concern you.

not
(adverb) used to make a sentence negative, to refuse something, or to deny something.

notable
(adjective) important or interesting, e.g. *With a few notable exceptions this trend has continued.*
notably (adverb).

[from a mistaken division of Middle English *an otch*]

note, notes, noting, noted
1 (noun) A note is a short letter.
2 A note is also a written piece of information that helps you to remember something, e.g. *I'll make a note of that.*
3 A note is also a banknote.
4 In music, a note is a musical sound of a particular pitch, or a written symbol that represents it.
5 A note is also an atmosphere, feeling, or quality, e.g. *There was a note of triumph in her voice... This was a good note on which to end.*
6 (verb) If you note a fact, you become aware of it or you mention it, e.g. *His audience, I noted, were looking bored.*
7 If you note something down, you write it down so that you will remember it.
8 (phrase) If you **take note** of something, you pay attention to it, e.g. *I had started taking note of political developments.*
[from Latin *nota* meaning 'mark' or 'sign']

note down
(phrasal verb) If you note something down, you write it down so that you will remember it.

notebook, notebooks
(noun) A notebook is a small book for writing notes in.

noted
(adjective) well-known and admired, e.g. *a noted American writer.*

noteworthy
(adjective) interesting or significant, e.g. *a noteworthy fact.*

nothing
(pronoun) not anything, e.g. *There's nothing to worry about.*

Similar words: zero, nought, nil, naught

notice, notices, noticing, noticed
1 (verb) If you notice something, you become aware of it.
2 (noun) Notice is attention or awareness, e.g. *Many cases have come to my notice.*
3 A notice is a written announcement.
4 Notice is also advance warning about something, e.g. *She could have done it if she'd had a bit more notice.*

按字母的先後次序排列 Alphabetical order

正如大部份參考書一般，英漢字典按字母的先後次序排列（alphabetical order）詞彙。你可用以下方法翻查 'nosy'：

1. 找出所有 'n' 的詞彙。

2. 按着第二個字母，找出 'no' 的詞彙，例如 no、nobility、noble……

3. 按着第三個字母，找出 'nos' 的詞彙，例如 nose、nosedive、nostalgia……

4. 按着第四個字母，找出 'nosy'（「好管閒事的」）！

提示一

要快速查字，可運用英漢字典中每頁頁首的引導詞（guide words），以得知頁上第一個與最後一個詞彙。若果要找的詞彙不在兩個引導詞的字母次序之列，那詞彙便不在那頁裏了。

發音 Pronunciation

字典除了提供詞意之外，通常也會教授詞彙的發音方法。展示詞彙發音有兩個常見方法：

- 音標（phonetic，採用羅馬字母）

- 國際音標（the International Phonetic Alphabet）

當發音是以音標表示時，相關詞彙便會以發音方法重新拼寫，按音節（syllables）分割開，並在重音上加上重音符號（stress mark [']）：

例子	音標
Norwegian（挪威人）	(*Nawwē'jun*)
alphabet（字母）	(*al'-fuh-bet*)

國際音標（the International Phonetic Alphabet）是一個含字母和符號的更準確系統，可使世上大部份語言（不只是英語）中的任何詞彙也能發音。

符號（'）放在重音音節的前方：

例子	國際音標
Norwegian（挪威人）	(nɔːˈwiːdʒən)
alphabet（字母）	(ˈælfəˌbɛt)

提示二

在一星期裏，每天用 10 分鐘時間練習準確翻開英漢字典中各字母的部份。翻對了就給自己 10 分，若是幾乎翻對、翻錯或大錯特錯等，便自行扣分。

提示三

為了節省空間，並非每個詞彙也是獨立分列在英漢字典裏的。例如，'leakage'（「滲漏」）可在 'leak'（「漏洞」）的名下找到；'sickness'（「患病」）可在 'sick'（「不適」）的名下找到。'Leak' 和 'sick' 是中心詞（headword）。

詞類 Parts of speech

任何一本優質字典也會按着詞類（parts of speech）列出意思。試看下例：

shake, shakes, shaking, shook, shaken
1 (verb) To shake something means to move it quickly from side to side or up and down.
2 (noun) If you give something a shake, you shake it.
3 (verb) If something shakes, it moves from side to side or up and down with small, quick movements.
4 If your voice shakes, it trembles because you are nervous or angry.
5 If something shakes you, it shocks and upsets you.
6 If something shakes your beliefs, it makes you doubt them.
7 When you shake your head, you move it from side to side in order to say 'no'.
8 (phrase) When you **shake hands** with someone, you grasp their hand as a way of greeting them.

Similar words: (sense 3) quake, quiver, tremble, shudder, tremor, shiver

你能找出 'shake' 以下的意思嗎？

(a) 名詞（noun）

(b) 及物動詞（transitive verb）

(c) 不及物動詞（intransitive verb）

fast, faster, fastest; fasts, fasting, fasted
1 (adjective and adverb) moving, doing something, or happening quickly or with great speed.
2 If a clock is fast, it shows a time that is later than the real time.
3 A fast film is very sensitive and can be used for taking photographs in low-light conditions.
4 A fast way of life involves a lot of enjoyable and expensive activities, e.g. *She wanted to move in the fast set.*
5 (adverb) Something that is held fast is firmly fixed.
6 (phrase) If you are **fast asleep**, you are in a deep sleep.
7 (adjective) Fast colours or dyes will not run or come out when wet.
8 (verb) If you fast, you eat no food at all for a period of time, usually for religious reasons.
9 (noun) A fast is a period of time during which someone does not eat food.

Similar words: (sense 1) quick, fleet, speedy, quickly, rapidly, swiftly

你能找出 'fast' 以下的意思嗎？

(a)形容詞（adjective），及其比較級（comparative）和最高級（superlative）

(b)副詞（adverb）

(c)不及物動詞（intransitive verb），（及其現在 [present] 和過去分詞 [past participles]）

短語和慣用語 Phrases and idioms

'That'll be fifty pounds.'
「合共 50 英鎊。」

Poor Charlie's paying through the nose. 可憐的查理花錢過多了。

每種語言也有一些用語是不能直接譯作另一語言的。這就是慣用語 (idioms)。

翻閱第一章「使用字典」印有中心詞 'nose' 的部份，試找出以下慣用語：

(a) to pay through the nose

(b) to turn up one's nose

答案：(a) 花錢過多

　　　(b) 蔑視某事物

用你自己的字典，查出以下各個特別的 (慣用語的) 意思：

(a) to be all ears

(b) feel your ears burning

(c) have an ear to the ground

(d) wet behind the ears

答案：(a) 細心傾聽

　　　(b) 認為別人在談論自己

　　　(c) 注意四周的動靜

　　　(d) 幼稚、經驗尚淺的

留意它們如何在句子中使用。

EXTRA Information 第三章進階寫作技巧有更多關於「慣用語」的介紹。

詞源 Word origins

找出詞彙的來源和它們如何演變成現今的英語意思是一件很有趣的事。大部份優質的字典也會為每個詞彙記載詞彙的原屬語言（original language），以及在該語言中的意思。

試看 'shillyshally' 一詞源自何方：

> **shillyshally, shillyshallies, shillyshallying, shillyshallied**
> (verb) If you shillyshally, you hesitate a lot and cannot make a decision.
> [from an 18th century expression '*to go, shill I, shall I*' meaning 'shall I or shan't I go']

字典中的附頁 Other dictionary pages

大部份字典在書首和書末也載有許多寶貴資料（如縮寫 [abbreviations]、詞彙列表 [word lists] 等等）。

許多字典會另以獨立部份記載：

- a list of common abbreviations
  常見縮寫列表
- a list of words and meanings too new to be in the main dictionary
  因太新而不適合收編在主流字典的詞彙列表
- a list of foreign words and phrases used, as they stand, in English
  在英語中使用的外來詞彙及短語列表
- a short history of the English language
  英語歷史簡介
- weights and measures
  度量衡表

另外，還有許多有趣的資料。

溫習 Revision

a, b, c, f, y...

A. 將以下詞語按字母的先後次序排列。

Random order	Alphabetical order
Horse	1.
Normal	2.
Monkey	3.
Animal	4.
Interesting	5.
Yacht	6.
Zebra	7.
Money	8.
Name	9.
Insect	10.

B. 細閱以下「match」一字在字典的解釋。找出它在下列句子屬於「noun」
（名詞）、「verb」（動詞），還是「phrase」（短語）。

> match
> i.　(noun) an organised game of sport
> ii.　(verb) to be the same as something else
> iii.　(phrase) meeting someone who you cannot beat as they are just
> 　　as good, or better than you

1. He had met his match in speed and skill. _____

2. We lost our hockey match against Hong Kong Rangers. _____

3. My dress matches my shoes. _____

4. She painted her room so it would match the rest of the flat. _____

5. They won their match at the weekend. _____

C. 將以下慣用語跟它們相對的意思配對。

Idiom	Meaning
1. see eye to eye	A. something that happens very rarely
2. once in a blue moon	B. wishing someone good luck
3. the last straw	C. when someone understands the situation well
4. speak of the devil	D. two people who agree with each other
5. on the ball	E. when something is very expensive
6. costs an arm and a leg	F. the final problem in a series of problems
7. Break a leg!	G. when someone who you have just been talking about arrives

D. 以下有關字典的句子是「True」（正確）還是「False」（錯誤）？

Sentence	True / False
1. Dictionaries are all the same size.	
2. Dictionaries tell you how to use the words in a sentence.	
3. Dictionaries tell you words which rhyme with each other.	
4. Dictionaries tell you the meanings of words.	

同義詞與反義詞 Synonyms and antonyms

同義詞（synonyms）意謂具有相同意思的詞彙。

同義詞（synonym）意謂具有相同意思的詞彙。

反義詞（antonym）意謂具有相反意思的詞彙。

用同義詞詞典找同義詞
Using a thesaurus to find synonyms

字典（dictionaries）收編同義詞（synonyms），時有反義詞（antonyms），以及許多其他相關的資料。同義詞詞典（thesaurus）是一本同樣有用的書，當中單單記載了有相同和相反意思的詞彙。

現代同義詞詞典在書中主頁按字母的先後次序（alphabetically）列出中心詞（headwords）。

visit *v.* **1.** be the guest of, call in, call on, drop in on (*Inf.*), go to see, inspect, look (someone) up, pay a call on, pop in (*Inf.*), stay at, stay with, stop by, take in (*Inf.*) **2.** afflict, assail, attack, befall, descend upon, haunt, smite, trouble **3.** *With* **on** *or* **upon** bring down upon, execute, impose, inflict, wreak ~*n.* **4.** call, sojourn, stay, stop
visitation 1. examination, inspection, vis~it **2.** bane, blight, calamity, cataclysm, catastrophe, disaster, infliction, ordeal, punishment, scourge, trial
visitor caller, company, guest, visitant

第一本同義詞詞典由羅傑彼得（Peter Mark Roget）編寫。此書在各個編碼部份列入同義詞，翻查時須先從書末的索引（index）找出詞彙，然後根據從索引所得的編號在主頁找出所需部份。

製造反義詞 Making antonyms

相反詞（opposites），即反義詞（antonyms），大多數由前綴（prefixes）加上詞根（root）造成：

im	+	*possible*	= *impossible*	（不可能）
non	+	*sense*	= *nonsense*	（廢話）
un	+	*usual*	= *unusual*	（不尋常）
il	+	*legal*	= *illegal*	（非法）
dis	+	*honest*	= *dishonest*	（不誠實）
in	+	*complete*	= *incomplete*	（不完整）

後綴 -less 也會用來造反義詞：

worth	+	*less*	= *worthless*	（無價值）
harm	+	*less*	= *harmless*	（無害）
brain	+	*less*	= *brainless*	（愚蠢）

Grammar Clinic

詞綴（affixes）如 in- 和 -less 並不一定造成相反意思的詞根。例如，'invaluable' 和 'priceless' 都解作貴重得無法定價的。'countless' 和 'innumerable' 均解作「多不勝數」。

使用每個新詞彙前，須常緊記要先翻查其意思。

溫習 Revision

A. 找出下列各組詞語是同義詞還是反義詞。在橫線上填上「synonym」(同義詞)
或「antonym」(反義詞)。

1. Tall and High _____

2. Brilliant and Great_____

3. Nice and Horrible _____

4. Light and Dark _____

5. Delicious and Tasty _____

6. Smooth and Rough _____

7. Ancient and Old _____

8. Boring and Exciting _____

9. Interesting and Fascinating _____

10. Clean and Dirty _____

My uncle is big and fat.

B. 圈出正確答案來完成句子。

1. The exam was (unpossible / impossible).

2. He was (uninterested / noninterested) in geography.

3. She was very (impolite / dispolite) to her teacher.

4. Tom didn't have to wear a tie as the event was extremely (unformal / informal).

5. He really wanted to be (unvisible / invisible) for a day.

6. It was (unnecessary / disnecessary) to bring extra chairs as not many people turned up.

C. 在橫線上填上前綴來完成句子。

1. He was very (_____ mature) and cried when he didn't get his own way.

2. He didn't like the performance. He felt very (_____ satisfied).

3. There was a gender (_____ balance) as there were more girls than boys.

4. She hated waiting, she was very (_____ patient).

5. Amy was busy all week and (_____ available) to go for lunch with Jim.

6. His actions were (_____ forgivable). He had betrayed her completely.

7. Adam was five years younger than the other competitors so he was at a (_____ advantage).

8. The puzzle was (_____ complete) — he hadn't finished it yet.

D. 圈出正確答案來完成句子。

1. The piece of jewelry was (priceless / nonprice).

2. The shopping list was (unend / endless).

3. The liquid was (colourless / discolour).

4. She thought that the lecture was completely (impoint / pointless).

5. The little dog was completely (harmless / disharm).

2 詞組與句子 Word Groups and the Sentence

A 句子 The sentence

B 標點符號 Punctuation

句子 The sentence

詞序 Word order

Dog bites postman

狗咬郵差

Postman bites Dog

郵差咬狗

詞序（order of words）可改變意思。

對於某些語言來説，句子中的詞序（order of words）並不重要，它並不會改變句子的意思。以英語這範疇來説，詞序與詞彙的位置卻很重要，更改任何一項，句子的意思也會隨之改變。

例如，看看以下句子怎樣隨詞序轉移而改變其意思：

The man walked his pet dog.

那男人帶他的寵物狗散步。

The pet dog walked his man.

那寵物狗帶牠的男人散步。

The dog walked his pet man.

那狗帶牠的寵物男人散步。

Walked pet the man dog his.

散步寵物那男人狗他。

正常的詞序 Normal word order

正常的詞序（normal word order）是：主語（subject）—— 動詞（verb）——實語（object）。

主語 Subject

主語（subject）即名詞（noun）、代詞（pronoun）或名詞短語（noun phrase），後接相關敍述：

***EXTRA** Information* 見第二章「名詞短語」。

My <u>mountain bike</u> has 16 gears.

我的爬山單車有 16 個傳動裝置。

The <u>video camera</u> helped to catch the shoplifter.

錄像機有助捉拿高買的人。

動詞 Verb

***EXTRA** Information* 有關動詞的資料見第一章「動詞」。

賓語 Object

賓語是受動詞（verb）的動作所影響的名詞（noun）或代詞（pronoun）：

The donkey ate the <u>carrot</u>.

驢子吃了那個蘿蔔。

Donna picked a <u>bunch of daisies</u>.

當娜採摘了一束雛菊。

My dog loves me.

我的狗愛我。

賓語（object）有兩種：

- 直接（direct）
- 間接（indirect）

直接賓語（direct object）即受動詞（verb）的動作直接影響的人或物：

Birds eat <u>worms</u>.

鳥兒吃蟲。

間接賓語（indirect object）即從動詞的動作，以及從動詞對賓語所作的動作，所受影響的人或物：

He gave <u>Lennie</u> a map.

他給了連尼一幅地圖。

He gave a map to <u>Lennie</u>.

他給了一幅地圖予連尼。

間接賓語（indirect object）常放在動詞和直接賓語之間（除了 'for' 或 'to' 出現的時候）。

More to Learn

謂語和補足語
Predicate and complement

謂語 Predicate

謂語（predicate）即句裏放在主語（subject）之後的其餘部份：

Tess thinks that Indian food is great.
得斯認為印度菜很好吃。

在上句中，'thinks that Indian food is great' 是謂語，當中包括了動詞和賓語。

補足語 Complement

補足語（complement）即句裏放在動詞或賓語之後的詞彙，用來使謂語完整（使句子的意思完整）：

I like nasty people to be punished.
我喜歡作惡的人受到懲罰。

在上句中，'to be punished' 是補足語。單靠左邊的 'I like nasty people' 是不能使句子意思完整的。

注意！

Yours（你的）、hers（她的）、ours（我們的）和 theirs（他們的）等物主代詞是從不加上撇號（apostrophe'）的。

若改變正常詞序，即主語（Subject）——動詞（Verb）——賓語（Object），意思也會隨之改變。最常見的改變是變成動詞（Verb）——主語（Subject）——賓語（Object），以製造疑問句（question）。

敘述句（Statement）：

主語 （Subject）	動詞 （Verb）	賓語 （Object）
You 你	*have never eaten* 從未吃過	*frog's legs.* 青蛙腳。

疑問句（Question）：

動詞 （Verb）	主語 （Subject）	賓語 （Object）
Have 你	*you never eaten* 有吃過	*frog's legs?* 青蛙腳嗎？

你也可改變詞序以製造效果。句子如：

'No!' was his definite answer.
「不！」是他的肯定答案。

可加強語氣至：

His answer was a definite 'No!'
他的答案是一個肯定的「不！」。

詞序和詞類
Word order and parts of speech

詞彙在句中的位置一般會決定其功能。試看看下列句子中 'round' 的功能。
試想想它在每例中屬甚麼詞類（part of speech），答案見本頁。

1. *The <u>round</u> of applause lasted for five minutes.*

一陣掌聲維持了五分鐘。

2. *Yachts <u>round</u> the buoy before the finish.*

帆船於終點前繞過浮標。

3. *The <u>round</u> table stood in Camelot.*

那圓桌放置在卡米樂城。

4. *We walked <u>round</u> to my Gran's.*

我們走回祖母家。

5. *You must run <u>round</u> the track.*

你必要繞着跑道走。

答案：

1. 名詞（noun，處於主語 [subject] 位置）

2. 動詞（verb，處於動詞位置）

3. 形容詞（adjective，位於名詞 'table' 的旁邊）

4. 副詞（adverb，位於動詞 'walked' 的旁邊）

5. 介詞（preposition，連起主語 'you' 和 'track'）

詞序和前置修飾語
Word order and modifiers

在句子中，任何詞彙若用作修飾（modifies，見「注意」部份）另一詞彙，兩者必須盡量靠近。在下列句子中，'only' 修飾不同詞彙，衍生出不同意思：

My only sister likes jazz.

我唯一的妹妹喜歡爵士樂。（我並無其他姐妹。）

My sister only likes jazz.

我妹妹喜歡爵士樂而已。（家中除我妹妹以外，無人喜歡爵士樂；或她只是喜歡爵士樂而已，並非達瘋癲程度。）

My sister likes only jazz.

我妹妹只喜歡爵士樂。（她並不喜歡其他音樂。）

My sister likes jazz only.

我妹妹只喜歡爵士樂。（與上例同，但此句子加強了語氣。）

―――――――――――――――――――― **注意！** ――――――――――――――――――――

前置修飾語 Modifiers

要「修飾」詞彙（'modify'），即另加意思在詞彙上。

在 'a red car'（「一輛紅色車」）這一短語中，'red' 一詞修飾 'car'，提供了更多有關那輛車的資料。

在 'We quickly scored 50 runs'（「我們很快便跑完 50 圈」）這句中，'quickly' 一詞修飾 'scored'。

前置修飾語（modifier）意指任何增加額外意思到另一詞彙上的詞彙。

短語 Phrases

短語（phrase）是指在句子中可作詞類（part of speech）使用的詞彙組合（group of words）。

名詞短語 Noun Phrase

名詞短語（noun phrase）是可作名詞用的詞彙組合：

Riding a bicycle requires skill.

騎自行車需要技巧。

上例短語 'Riding a bicycle'（「騎自行車」）構成主語（subject），同時可作名詞用。

還記得 'What（甚麼）?' 的疑問句是辨認名詞的方法之一嗎？

***EXTRA** Information* 見第一章「辨別名詞：怎樣辨認名詞」。

名詞加上其形容詞（無論是單詞或短語）也當作名詞短語（noun phrase）：

That barking dog from next door keeps me awake at night.

鄰家那隻吠叫的狗兒令我不能入睡。

形容詞短語 Adjective Phrase

形容詞短語（adjective phrase）是可作形容詞（adjective）用的詞彙組合：

The man with the tall white hat is the chef.

那個戴着白色高帽的男人是廚師。

上例短語 'with the tall white hat'（「戴着白色高帽的」）指出是哪個男人，因此當作形容詞用。

還記得 'Which（哪些）?' 的疑問句是辨認形容詞的方法之一嗎？

***EXTRA** Information*　見第一章「辨別形容詞：怎樣辨認形容詞」。

動詞短語 Verb Phrases

動詞短語（verb phrase）是構成動詞（verb）的詞彙組合：

I shall be going to town tomorrow.

我明天會到市鎮去。

上例助動詞（auxiliary verb）'shall be'（「會」）與現在分詞（present participle）'going'（「去」）是必須的，用來表示作發生在將來：

還記得 'What does（or did）the subject do（主語做〔或做過〕甚麼）?' 的疑問句是辨認動詞的方法之一嗎？

***EXTRA** Information*　見有關「辨別詞類—用疑問方法」。

More to Learn

短語動詞 Phrasal verbs

動詞（verb）常跟副詞（adverb）連用構成某特定意思，如下例的 'up'：

Please shut up! 請住嘴！

上例短語動詞（phrasal verb）'shut up' 意即「肅靜」，跟 'to shut'（「關上」）的正常意思有很大分別。

短語動詞多得數以百計，包括：turn out（關上）、write off（注銷）、step up（使增加）、 square up（付帳）、 polish off（迅速完成）、run down（耗盡）。試想出更多例子。

副詞短語 Adverb Phrases

副詞短語（adverb phrase）是可作副詞用的詞彙組合：

Gran was snoring <u>in bed</u> last night.

婆婆昨晚在床上打鼾。

短語 'in bed'（「在床上」）描述動詞發生的地方。

還記得 'Where（哪裏）?' 的疑問句是辨認副詞的方法之一嗎？

***EXTRA** Information*　見第一章「辨別形容詞：怎樣辨認形容詞」。

分句 Clauses

含有動詞（verb）的短語（phrase）就稱為分句（clause）。分句構成句子（sentences）的部份。

分句（clause）主要有三個種類：

- 名詞分句（noun clauses）
- 形容詞分句（adjective clauses）
- 副詞分句（adverb clauses）

名詞分句 Noun clauses

在以下句子中，畫上底線的詞組包含動詞 'knew'（「認識」），並構成了動詞 'was' 的主語（subject）：

<u>*What my elder brother knew about pop music*</u> *was next to nothing.*

我哥哥對流行音樂幾乎一竅不通。

在以下句子中，畫上底線的詞組包含動詞 'are going'（「要往」），並構成了動詞 'to know'（「知道」）的賓語（object）：

I want to know <u>where you are going</u>.

我想知道你要往哪裏去。

形容詞分句 Adjective clauses

在下例中，畫上底線的分句指明哪個是所談及的男人，並可作形容詞（adjective）用。這是分句，因為當中包含了動詞 'wearing'（「戴着」）。

The man <u>who is wearing the purple bobble hat</u> is my dad.

那個戴着紫色絨球帽的男人是我爸爸。

形容詞分句（adjective clauses）有兩種：

- 限制性（defining）
- 非限制性（non-defining）

要指明所談及的名詞，限制性分句（defining clauses）是必要的：

The man <u>who is wearing the purple bobble hat</u> is my dad.

那個戴着紫色絨線球帽的男人是我爸爸。

非限制性分句 *(non-defining clauses)* 只用作提供額外資料，對句子的意思並無關鍵影響：

Most dads, <u>who don't usually wear purple bobble hats</u>, aren't as crazy as mine.

大多數父親，即通常也不戴紫色絨線球帽的那些，並不如我父親般瘋狂。

注意！

非限制性分句（non-defining clauses）必要括在逗號（commas）或括號（brackets）之內。

副詞分句 Adverb clauses

副詞分句（adverb clauses）有八種：

- 時間：回答疑問句 'When（何時）?'：

He sent a fax <u>as soon as he arrived</u>.
他到步後便立刻傳真出去。

- 地點：回答疑問句 'Where（何地）?'：

The boy stood <u>where the burning deck was coolest</u>.
那男孩站在起火甲板最涼的地方。

- 原因：回答疑問句 'Why（為甚麼）?'：

The jockey was wearing pyjamas <u>because the horse always came in so late</u>.
騎師還穿着睡衣，皆因馬兒常蹣跚來遲。

- 目的：回答疑問句 'For what purpose（為何目的）?'：

He killed his parents <u>so he could watch 'Orphans' Picnic'</u>.
他謀殺雙親，為了看《孤兒們的野餐》。

- 結果：回答疑問句 'With what results（結果如何）?'：

My house was so scruffy <u>that some vandals broke in and decorated it</u>.
我的房子因太凌亂，結果有些恣意破壞公物的人偷偷進來並裝飾它一番。

- 條件：回答疑問句 'Under what conditions or circumstances（在甚麼條件或情況下）?'：

<u>If you steal that calendar</u>, you'll get 12 months!
如果你偷了那個月曆，你就可得到 12 個月了！

- 讓步：句子常以 'though'（「雖然」）、'although'（「雖然」），或類似的連詞（conjunctions）開首，並指出 'granting certain circumstances'（「承認某些特定的情況」）：

Though I tried to play the piano, I failed miserably.

儘管我努力嘗試彈鋼琴，但卻有心無力。

- 比較：這類分句拿兩樣物件或主意互相比較：

The food is not as good <u>as it used to be</u>.

現在的食物不及以往的美味。

More to Learn

主句及從句 Main and subordinate clauses

在一個含有兩個分句（clauses）的句子（sentence）裏，常有一個是主句（main clause），另一個是從句（subordinate clause）：

　　　　從句　　　　　　　　　　　主句

As I was going to Paddock Wood,
當我往柏度林時，

　　　　　　　　　　I met a girl named Suzie Hood.
　　　　　　　　　　遇見一位名叫胡蘇時的女子。

第二分句才是主句因為它可獨立成句，但第一分句卻無法獨立成句。

然而，有時候主句會斷開，把分句放在中間：

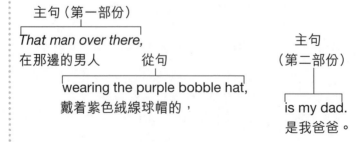

　　主句（第一部份）

That man over there,
在那邊的男人　　　　從句　　　　　　　（第二部份）

　　　　　wearing the purple bobble hat,
　　　　　戴着紫色絨線球帽的，　　　*is my dad.*
　　　　　　　　　　　　　　　　是我爸爸。

　　　　　　　　　　　　主句

句子種類 Types of sentences

'That's cool!'

「了不起！」

'Yes, but what is it?'

「對，但究竟是甚麼來的？」

句子（sentences）有不同種類。

句子有五種：

- 陳述句（statements）
- 疑問句（questions）
- 命令句（commands）
- 感歎句（exclamations）
- 祝願句／假設句（wishes）

陳述句 Statements

陳述句（statements）的詞序是主語（Subject）—— 動詞（Verb）——賓語（Object）：

Cows eat grass.

牛吃草。

疑問句 Questions

疑問句（questions）的詞序是動詞（Verb）—— 主語（Subject）—— 賓語
（Object）：

Do elephants eat spaghetti?

大象吃意大利粉嗎？

命令句 Commands

命令句（commands）也稱為 'imperatives'（「祈使句」）：

Don't swallow that spanner!

別吞掉那扳手！

感歎句 Exclamations

感歎句（exclamations）是用作感嘆（interjections）的短語（phrases）：

What an idiot I've been!

我真是個傻瓜！

祝願句／假設句 Wishes

一致金律（the concord rule）有時候並不適用於這類句子，因為動詞另有
特別用法，稱為「虛擬語氣」（'subjunctive mood'）：

EXTRA *Information* 見第一章 More to Learn 有關「一致金律」。

If only I were old enough, I would join the air force.

要是我夠年長，我會加入空軍。

May you have a long and happy life.

但願你長壽快樂。

造句 The construction of sentences

「牛奶對身體有益『因為』它可使骨骼強壯。」

並非所有句子也是短句，這並列句（compound sentence）便是例子之一。

簡單句 Simple sentences

可獨立理解，只含一個動詞而已，並非全是短句！

Most dogs are friendly.
大部份狗兒都很友善。

Did you hear the one about the Englishman, the Irishman and the Scotsman?
你聽過那個關於英國人、愛爾蘭人和蘇格蘭人的笑話嗎？

Boiling with rage at the defendant's impertinence and controlling himself with difficulty, the judge ordered the court to be cleared.
法官對被告人的無禮感到怒髮衝冠、難以自制，於是下令退堂。

並列句 Compound sentences

運用連接詞（conjunction），如 'and'（「和」）、'but'（「但是」）、'because'（「因為」）等或合適的標點符號（punctuation），組合兩句或以上的簡單句（simple sentences）所構成的句子：

EXTRA *Information* 見第二章「標點符號」。

Jack fell down and broke his crown.

傑克跌倒並弄穿了頭。

Jack fell down, broke his crown and was carried off yelling.

傑克跌倒、弄穿了頭，被抬走時還大喊大叫。

留意上例並不用重複「傑克」三次，因為每句分句（clause）都是以「傑克」作主語（subject）的。

由單一分句加上一個或以上的名詞分句（noun clauses）、形容詞分句（adjective clauses）或副詞分句（adverb clauses）組成：

主句（Main clause）   從句（Subordinate clause）

You ought to be on TV,   *so we could turn you off!*
你應該在電視上出現，   那麼我們便可關掉你！

'You ought to be on TV'（「你應該在電視上出現」）是主句，其餘都是從句。

EXTRA *Information* 見第二章「More to Learn」。

提示一

多用複合句（complex sentence）來改善寫作風格（writing style）。

- **差劣**：*I was eager to get up this morning. A carpet of dazzling white snow lay thickly outside my window.*

  今早我急不及待起床。窗外鋪了一層厚厚的閃爍耀眼的白雪。

- **較佳**：*Because a carpet of dazzling white snow lay outside my window, I was eager to get up this morning.*

  因為窗外鋪了一層厚厚的閃爍耀眼的白雪，今早我急不及待起床。

以上第一個版本的兩句簡單句（simple sentences）並無展示出兩句之間的因果關係，但第二個版本的複合句（complex sentence）則展示了。

提示二

為文風加力，放主句（main clause）在最後：

- **起強調作用**：*Until you stop smoking, don't complain about your cough!*

  在你還沒有戒煙之前，別抱怨自己咳嗽！

- **起懸疑作用**：*In the very doorway on the street where Sikes was to have handed over the stolen goods, there stood a policeman.*

  在西斯打算轉交賊臟的街道出入口旁，正正站着一名警員。

More to Learn

鬆散句、完全句和平衡句
Loose, periodic and balanced sentences

鬆散句（loose sentence）意謂主句（main clause）開首的句子（即在任何從句 [subordinate clauses] 之先）：

Look both ways, if you want to stay safe.
看守兩方，如果你想平安無事的話。

完全句（periodic sentence）意謂以主句或動詞結束的句子。（美國人多用 'period' 一詞代替 'full stop'[句號或腳點]）：

If you want to stay safe, look both ways.
如果你想平安無事的話，看守兩方。

平衡句（balanced sentence）意謂含有兩個或以上具同樣重要的分句的句子：

Emperor Nero fiddled while Rome burned.
當羅馬焚燒時，尼祿王正在胡混。

溫習 Revision

A. 按正確的詞序排列，寫出各句。

1. the table is pen on the	
2. ate he an apple	
3. went she to the zoo	
4. talk interesting was the	
5. was food the delicious	
6. for you good is fruit	
7. black the was expensive very dress	
8. fantastic was their holiday	

B. 找出下列各句有底線的詞語屬於「subject」（主語）、「verb」（動詞），還是「object」（賓語）。

1. The dog ate the <u>bone</u>. _____

2. My <u>laptop</u> is broken. _____

3. I got a new <u>job</u>. _____

4. The kind boy <u>helped</u> the old man.
   _____

5. He <u>cooked</u> and amazing meal.
   _____

6. My <u>mobile phone</u> is really old. _____

C. 將以下各陳述句改寫為疑問句。

Statement	Question
1. The water was cold.	
2. The ice-cream was delicious.	
3. You have been to Thailand.	
4. You have seen the new school building.	
5. He has finished his homework.	
6. The people are friendly.	

D. 找出「cross」在以下各句屬於「noun」（名詞）、「verb」（動詞），還是「adjective」（形容詞）。

1. He crossed the road. _____

2. Jesus died on the cross.

3. The dog was a cross between a Labrador and an Alsatian. _____

4. Put a cross next to the correct answer. _____

5. She crossed her arms. _____

6. She was really cross with him. _____

E. 圈出正確的分句來完成句子。

1. I didn't tell him where I was / where was I.

2. I think is she / she is from England.

3. Is it true what they say / what did they say about you?

4. The man who was ill / was ill looked extremely pale.

5. The person is who / who is in the car is my sister.

6. Before / Since the show, they went to a restaurant.

7. Although / After the film, they went home.

8. He was wearing a jumper because / as soon as he was cold.

9. Since / If you come early, you will get a free drink.

F. 找出以下各句屬於「statement」(陳述句)、「question」(疑問句)、「command」(命令句)、「exclamation」(感歎句),還是「wish」(祝願句／假設句)。

Sentences	Types of Sentences
1. Trees are green.	
2. Do dogs eat grass?	
3. How silly of me!	
4. Don't sit there!	
5. If I was taller, I'd be a model.	
6. What a horrible day!	
7. May you have a long and happy marriage.	
8. Eat quickly!	
9. Are you going on holiday?	

G. 用連接詞將兩個句子改為一句。

1. Tom fell over. He hurt his knee.

   _____

2. Emma went to the market. She bought some vegetables.

   _____

3. Lynn likes apples. She doesn't like bananas.

   _____

4. She went to sleep. She was tired.

   _____

5. He has been to Thailand. He hasn't been to Cambodia.

   _____

I am clever *and* funny.

標點符號 Punctuation

標點符號（punctuation）很重要。放標點符號在字裏行間可使文章更易讀和更易理解，而正確的標點符號更可改變文章意思。以下兩例詞彙相同，但意思卻迥然不同：

What do you think? I will feed you for nothing!

你意思怎樣？我會無條件地養活你！（一個好的待遇）

What! Do you think I will feed you for nothing!

甚麼！你以為我會無條件地養活你嗎！（並非好的待遇！）

結束句子 Ending a sentence

Jack and Emma
傑克與愛瑪

... are friends!
是朋友！

句子以標點符號（punctuation mark）結束。

差不多所有句子皆以下列標點符號作結：

- 句號（full stop）：（.）

This sentence ends with a full stop and here it comes now.
這句句子以句號作結，它現即出現。

- 問號（question mark）：（？）

What goes 'Ha-ha plonk'?
甚麼東西會發出「哈哈砰」的聲響？

- 感歎號（exclamation mark）：（！）

What a fantastic joke!
真是一個有趣的笑話！

注意！

只有直接疑問句（direct questions）才會以問號（question mark）結束。
以下句子並非直接疑問句，因此不需使用問號：

I asked what went 'Ha-ha plonk'.
我問甚麼東西會發出「哈哈砰」的聲響。

More to Learn

如問句的意思具感歎（exclamation）成份多於疑問（question）成份，那就應以感歎號（exclamation mark）結束：

Who do you think you are! What about that!
你以為自己是誰！那又如何！

某些句子結尾是較為少見的：

- 直接引語（direct speech）：（' 或 "）

	若句子以直接引語（direct speech）結束（某人實際所説的話），那麼引號（quotation marks）通常放在標點符號之後，以結束句子。

	She said nervously, 'I'm just a harmless pupil. Why are you confusing me with all this grammar?'

	她緊張地説：「我只是一個無辜的學生。為甚麼你要用這些語法來為難我？」

	EXTRA *Information*　見第二章「説話中的標點符號」。

- 破折號（dash）：（—）

	當某人在跟另一個人説話、突然的念頭或事情等打斷了，那就使用破折號（dash）。

	'The cabin's on fire and the ship's going to —' Abruptly, the commander's voice ceased. A deathly silence spread over Mission Control.

	「船艙着火了，船也將 ——」突然間，船長不作聲。一片寂靜蔓延至整個指揮部。

	留意破折號代替了句號（full stop），而上例是不需句號的。

- 省略號（dots）：（...）

	若想讀者幻想其餘動作或表示時間流逝，在句末可用三點（three dots）：

	Between us we swung the body of the murdered crook far out into the river. The evil eyes of an alligator glinted greedily...

	我們兩人合力拋那遭謀殺的騙子屍體進河中。鱷魚邪惡的眼睛貪婪地閃亮着……

	這三點的正統名稱是 'ellipsis'（「省略號」）。

句子中的標點符號 Punctuation within sentences

標點符號（punctuation）給讀者在句中歇息的機會。

逗號（ , ）The comma

逗號（commas）用在讀者需停頓的位置。下列情況必要使用逗號：

- 在清單（list）中分開詞彙（words）和短語（phrases）：

My newly bought bargain car had leather seats, electric windows, central door locking, air-conditioning — but no brakes. Slowly, silently, smoothly, it rolled into the river.

我剛買回來的廉價車裝有皮革椅子、電動窗、中央門鎖系統、空調——但無剎車器。它慢慢地、靜悄悄地、暢順地滑進河裏。

- 在句子（sentence）中分開詞彙和短語：

The car dealer, Ted Smart, watched it all with a sly smile. He told me, with a casual shrug, that he wouldn't refund my money.

車商司馬達奸狡的一笑置之。他漫不經心地聳了聳肩，跟我説他不會退款。

- 在句子中分開分句（clauses）：

He added, while my face turned a shade of purple, that I was a fool.
當我臉色發紫時，他還說我是個蠢才。

I tried to reason with him, but Smart just went on grinning.
我嘗試跟他理論，但司馬只是繼續咧嘴而笑。

然而，若兩句分句的主語是相同的話，那就毋須用逗號：

I tried to stop myself but just couldn't help punching him on the nose.
我嘗試控制自己，但卻忍不住向他的鼻子打了一拳。

- 以名字稱呼說話對象時：

Pick yourself up, Mr Smart! How do you like that, Smarty!
站起來吧，司馬先生！你感覺如何呀，司馬仔！

- 使用修飾整句句子的副詞（adverbs）和副詞短語（adverb phrases）時（詞彙如 however [但是]、nevertheless [然而]、therefore [因此]、of course [當然]、in fact [事實上]、for instance [例如] 等等）：

Of course, Smart didn't stay down for long.
當然，司馬很快便站起來。

- 在直接引語（direct speech）中：

'OK,' *he muttered,* 'you can have your money back.'
「好，」他咕嚕地說：「你可取回退款。」

EXTRA *Information* 見第二章有關「直接引語」。

分號（ ;) The semi-colon

分號（semi-colon）現在比以前較少用，但它卻很有用。下列情況可使用分號：

- 不使用連接詞（conjunction）把兩句或以上的簡單句子（simple sentences）連結起來，只有當第二句子與第 句子之間存在着很強的連繫時才可使用分號：

The bandit, Sal Elastico, left the court for the cells; he knew the way. The robber had hoped for probation; instead, Elastico was going down for a long stretch.

土匪艾拉迪加沙離開法庭往監獄去；他懂得路。這強盜希望得到緩刑；但事與願遺，他將要坐很長時間的牢。

- 當一連串的從句（subordinate clauses）皆以同一動詞（verb）連繫時：

At yesterday's assembly, the headteacher said that she was particularly pleased that the table manners at lunchtime were much more polite; that the school team had won their soccer match; that the behaviour in the playground had improved.

在昨天的集會上，主任說她很高興學生在午飯時的餐桌禮儀比以往更得體、校隊在足球比賽中取得勝利，以及在操場上的操行改善了。

以上每句分句都以動詞 'said' 連繫着。

- 當清單中的獨立項目已需用上逗號時，便要使用分號把項目分隔開：

The four disciples closest to Jesus were: Peter, known also by the names Simon and Cephas; James, the first of the disciples to be martyred; John, James's brother, sometimes referred to as 'the disciple whom Jesus loved'; and Andrew, Simon Peter's brother.

四位耶穌最親的門徒是：彼得，又名西門和磯法；雅各，第一個殉道的門徒；約翰，雅各的哥哥，時稱「耶穌喜愛的門徒」；以及安得烈，西門彼

得的哥哥。

• 當在平衡的句子（balanced sentences）中，兩句分句使用同一動詞，而第二句的動詞可省去時：

My grandad keeps ferrets; my grandma poisonous snakes.

我的祖父飼養雪貂；祖母則養毒蛇。

冒號（:）The colon

冒號（colon）常表示接下來的是例子、解釋或清單。可在下列情況使用：

• 介紹清單或例子時（如現例）

• 分開兩個陳述句子（statements），而第二句用作解釋第一句時：

Many workers were late this morning: the fog caused delays on the roads.

今早有很多工人遲到：霧氣延誤了交通。

• 　介紹很長的引文（quotation）時

• 　在劇本（plays）中標示説話

***EXTRA** Information* 見第二章有關「戲劇中的標點符號」。

破折號（ — ）The dash

英語專家不常接受破折號（dash），但它很有用。
破折號主要用在記錄英語口語，它可用來表示：

- 突然改變主意：

Let's talk about bananas — no, perhaps we'll cover pineapples first.

來談談香蕉——不好，我們還是先說鳳梨。

- 插入句中強而有力和額外的意思（如那些不足以用逗號表示其力量的意思）：

My advice — if you will pardon my bluntness — is to think before you open your mouth.

我的意見是——恕我直言——說話前先要三思！

Jack was angry — nay, furious — at being interrupted in such a rude way.

傑克因遭無禮打擾而氣憤——不，是怒髮衝冠才對。

- 冗長的猶豫：

Well — er — all I can say is — er — thanks very much!

呀——呀——我可說的是——呀——非常感激你！

省略號（ ... ）The ellipsis

除了用來結束句子之外，也可在句中使用三點以表示詞彙給刻意省略了。
省略號（ellipses）通常用於重複引文時：

We will fight them on the beaches... we shall fight in the hills; we shall never surrender.

我們會在海灘上跟他們對戰……我們會在山上作戰；我們永不言敗。

括號（ ）Brackets

括號（brackets）用來括着句中事後想起的詞彙或詞組，或用來解釋句中意思：

The referee (my Dad) made some unfortunate decisions. He sent me off (even though he knew Mum would be furious with him when we got home).

那位球證（我的父親）下了錯誤的決定。他判罰我出場（即使他知道回家後媽媽會對他大發雷霆）。

注意！

另外還有三種方法可以括起句中或段中的詞彙或詞組：

• 逗號（, ）：

Mr Jones, the professional fire-eater, lives next door.

鍾斯先生，那個專門表演吞火的人，就住在隔壁。

• 方括號 [ ]，用於在引文時加插原文沒有提供的解釋：

'England expects,' he [Nelson] signalled, 'every man to do his duty.'

他 [尼爾森] 示意：「英國要求每人也要各盡其職。」

• 破折號（ — ）：

The film star threw a wobbly — or rather a tantrum — because her champagne was warm.

那電影明星發怒——應該說是大發脾氣——因為她的香檳是暖的。

詞彙裏的標點符號 Punctuation within words

撇號（apostrophes）代替缺漏的字母。

連字符號（-）Hyphens

連字符號（hyphens）：(-)

- 用來連結兩個或以上的詞彙，形成一個新的複合詞（compound word）：

  sun-tanned（曬黑的）　　*up-to-date*（最新的）
  a ten-year-old（一個十歲的兒童）

- 用來分隔開前綴（prefix）與詞根（root word），以避免難看的字母組合：

  co-ordinate（協調）　　*pre-eminent*（傑出的）
  de-ice（除去冰）　　*will-less*（不願意的）

- 用來避免跟現存的詞彙混淆：

  re-cover（換上新的套子）　≠　*recover*（復原）

· 用於跟大楷字母（capital letters）合併時：

U-turn（掉頭）　　　　　　　*T-junction*（丁字路口）
un-American（非美國的）　　　*pre-Victorian*（維多利亞時代前）

──────────────── **注意！** ────────────────

使用連字符號（hyphens）的規則會隨着時代改變，因此要經常參考既優質又能追上時代的字典。

撇號（ ' ）Apostrophes

撇號（apostrophes）：

· 用來標示省略的字母：

can't	= *cannot*	（不能）
won't	= *will not*	（不會）
let's	= *let us*	（讓我們來）
I'll	= *I will*	（我會）
that's	= *that is*	（那是）

· 用來表示物主（possession）：

the girl's pens　　≠　*the girls' pens*
（女孩的筆）　　　　　（女孩們的筆）

the princess's jewels　≠　*the princesses' jewels*
（公主的珠寶）　　　　　（公主們的珠寶）

the woman's eyes　≠　*the women's eyes*
（女人的眼睛）　　　　（女士們的眼睛）

||||||||||||||||||||||||||||||||||||||| **注意！** |||||||||||||||||||||||||||||||||||||||||||||||||

正確放置物主撇號（possessive apostrophes）是很容易的事，絕不需要理會物主是單數（singular）還是複數（plural），只要問自己：「[物件名稱] 屬於何人（或何物）？」跟着直接加撇號在物主之後便可。

例一：The dog's bone.　那隻狗的骨頭。

　　　（有一隻狗）

問題：那骨頭屬於誰？

答案：那隻狗。現可在 'dog' 之後加上撇號。

例二：The dogs' bone.　那羣狗的骨頭。

　　　（有兩隻或以上的狗）

問題：那骨頭屬於誰？

答案：那羣狗。現可在 'dogs' 之後加上撇號。

容易極了！

另有一些使用撇號（apostrophe）的規則：

1. 若名詞後加 's 會變得難聽或難以發音，要刪去 s：

　　Moses' sister 摩西的姐姐（*Moses's* 很難聽）

　　Brutus' wife 布托斯的妻子（不寫 *Brutus's*）

2. 撇號用來表示時間持續：

　　in a week's time 在一星期內

　　two weeks' holiday 兩星期的假期

　　跟應在何處插入撇號的規則相同。

EXTRA Information　見第二章「詞彙裏的標點符號」。

3. 撇號用來為字母及沒有複數形式的詞彙標示複數：

p's and q's　*p's* 和 *q's*

if's and but's「假若」和「但是」

There are too many and's in that sentence.
句中太多「和」字了。

句號或腳點（.）Full stops

句號或腳點（full stop）常用於表示詞彙縮寫：

a.m.（上午）　　　　　*Feb.*（二月）　　　*etc.*（等等）
Man. City（曼徹斯特市）　　*approx.*（大約）

但若詞首和詞尾的字母已包括在縮寫內，那便不必使用句號或腳點：Dr（醫生）、maths（數學）、Man. Utd（曼聯）、Mrs（太太）

説話中的標點符號 Punctuation of speech

'OK class... it's home time,' said Mrs Sluggit.

「好了，同學們⋯⋯是時候回家了。」斯理結太太説。

引號（quotation marks）括起說話者的話。

引號（quotation marks [' ' 或 " "]），又名倒轉的逗號（inverted commas）或說話符號（speech marks），用於書面上標示說話者確實的說話。這樣的說話稱為直接引語（direct speech）。若是用手寫出來的話，便用雙引號（double quotation marks [" "]）。

More to Learn

在英國出版的書籍常用單引號，不用雙引號。相反，在美國出版的書籍則常用雙引號。

引號的使用規則如下：

1. 引號只括着確實的説話：

用引號：*Fiona said, 'I'm hungry.'*
　　　　費安娜説：「我肚餓。」

（這是直接引語 [direct speech]。）

不用引號：*Fiona said that she was hungry.*
　　　　　　費安娜説她肚餓。

（這是被轉述引語 [reported speech]。）

2. 若引語中途給説話者自己的引語打斷，説話重新開始時無需使用大階：

'I'm so hungry,' said Fiona, 'that I could eat the fridge door.'
費安娜説：「我肚子餓得可吃下冰箱門。」

3. 引號關上或重開之前必定在標點符號的停頓位置，通常是逗號（comma）或者句號（full stop）；問號（question mark）或者感歎號（exclamation mark）。因此下例中 'metal' 之後有逗號，'healthy' 之後有句號：

'Eating metal,' said David, 'is not very healthy.'
大衛説：「吃金屬不太健康。」

4. 每次轉換説話者也要另開一個新段落，這可使説話者顯而易見：

'I'll leave the fridge door then,' said Fiona.
費安娜説：「那我就不吃冰箱門吧。」

'You could always try chewing the cupboard,' put in David.
大衛插嘴説：「你隨時都可嘗試咀嚼櫥櫃呀。」

'No thanks!'
「別客氣了。」

'Suit yourself,' said David. 'I quite like a juicy shelf now and then.'
大衛説：「隨便你吧。我偶爾也蠻喜歡美味的架。」

（留意即使大衞説出的句子已完結，'yourself' 之後也用逗號。腳點只在作者寫出的句子完結時才出現，即在 'David' 之後。）

更多進階程度的規則 More advanced rules

5. 若一位説話者連續説出長達幾個段落的話，那就在開始新段落時重開引號，但切勿在引語完結之前關上引號。

6. 若説話者引述另一人的説話，使用單引號（若以手寫出來的時候）括着説話者引述別人的話：

"I distinctly heard the starter say 'Go'," said the athlete who had left his blocks too soon.

「我清楚聽見發令員説『跑』。」太早起跑的運動員説。

常用單引號的書籍會用雙引號來括着説話中的引語。

戲劇中的標點符號 Punctuation of plays

DOCTOR [cheerfully]: My word!
GRIMBLE [anxiously]: Is that me?

醫生［興高采烈地］：不得了！
京寶［憂心地］：你在說我嗎？

為了避免使用太多引號（speech marks），劇本（plays）有一套特定的標點符號（punctuation）使用方法。下例是一段劇本摘錄：

A doctor's waiting room. DOCTOR, a young cheerful man, enters R. GRIMBLE, a middle-aged patient, is seated L (Left) in front of the doctor's desk.

候診室內。醫生，一名笑顏開的年輕人，從台右進入。京寶，一名中年病人，面向醫生桌在台左坐着。

DOCTOR (sitting down): Now, how are your broken ribs coming along, Mr Grimble?

醫生（邊坐邊說）：京寶先生，你折斷的肋骨復原得怎樣？

GRIMBLE (anxiously): Well, I keep getting this stitch in my side!

京寶（憂心忡忡地）：啊，我旁邊身軀常感到刺痛！

DOCTOR (cheerfully): Good, that shows the bones are knitting!

醫生（興高采烈地）：好，那表示你的骨在修補中呀！

規則如下：

1. 佈景（setting）及演員位置（position of actors）的描述以斜體字（italics）印製。（若是手寫稿，便用方括號 [ ] 括着。）

2. 角色（characters）名稱以大階（capital letters）寫出。

3. 所有動作（movement）及聲音（voice）指示都寫在括號（brackets）內。

4. 除非角色或者人物引述直接引語（direct speech），否則切勿用引號（quotation marks）。

More to Learn

數學上的標點符號
Punctuation in maths

常用逗號（commas）或空位（spaces）使人容易理解巨大數目：

12,345,063 或 12 345 063

它們每逢三個數位（digits）加插一次。由個位數從右至左開始計算。

小數點（decimal point）永遠放在個位數（units）與小數十位（tenths）之間，印刷出來就如腳點（full stop）般：
104.25

寫出來，就要寫在數字高度的一半位置：
104·25

溫習 Revision

'I'm so happy?!@,.'

A. 填上正確標點符號。

1. Are you going to work today _____

2. What a beautiful summer's day _____

3. Who does he think he is _____

4. He was so excited to sleep in his new _____ comfy bed.

5. They walked slowly into the pitch black cave. Suddenly they heard a strange noise _____

6. My opinion _____ if you don't mind me giving it _____ is that you should wear the black dress.

B. 圈出正確答案來完成文章。

Ben and Mary were packing for their holiday.

(1. " / ') I think I'll bring an extra towel,' said Ben, '(2. in case / In case) the first one gets dirty (3. , / .)'

'Good idea (4. , / .)' said Mary. '(5. did / Did) you pack the sun cream?'

'Yes, it's in my hand luggage (6. , / .)' (7. Replied / replied) Ben.

'Great. It's meant to be hot, so I think we will need a lot!'

'We can always buy more if we run (8. — / …)'

'I'm so excited!' Mary squealed before Ben could finish his sentence. 'I'm going to take a look at the guide book again tonight and make sure we aren't missing anything.'

'Good plan!' said Ben.

C. 在橫線上填上冒號、分號、破折號或括號。如果不需要標點符號，則留空白。

1. Many people were late_____ the traffic was very bad.

2. Mrs Lee _____ my teacher _____ doesn't let us talk in class.

3. My mum doesn't like it _____ actually hates it _____ when I don't wash the dishes

4. He left quickly _____ he wanted to get home.

5. I divided my coins into two piles _____ silver ones and gold ones.

6. I don't like going to the beach _____ because I hate getting sand in my shoes.

7. Let's go shopping _____ actually, let's go and eat first.

8. Her hair was soaking wet _____ she had forgotten to pack her umbrella.

9. The shoes _____ made of leather _____ were extremely expensive.

10. My piano teacher was happy that I had practiced my scales _____ improved my pieces _____ bought my new books _____ passed my theory test.

D. 為下列句子加上連字符號、撇號或句號。

1. The womans eyes were beautiful.	
2. He woke up at 7 am this morning.	
3. I wont be able to come tonight.	
4. He was very unBritish.	
5. In a weeks time, Ill be on holiday!	

3 進階寫作技巧
Advanced Writing Skills

A 段落 **The paragraph**

B 語言的特別運用 **Special uses of language**

段落 The paragraph

段落（paragraph）即指與某題目相關的一組句子。在正式的文章中，段落中的每一個句子（sentence）也必須跟這個主旨（main idea）相關。

主題句（**topic sentence**）表明主旨（**main idea**）

而主旨則包含例子（**example**）及解釋（**explanation**）。

每個段落（paragraph）必須有主旨（main idea）。

主題句 Topic sentence

為文章編寫段落，每一個段落也應有「主題句」（'topic sentence'），以清楚表明段落的中心思想。主題句通常是段落的開首句子，但這並不是規定的。故事（stories）或敍述文（narrative）的段落則不一定需要主題句。

段落種類 Types of paragraphs

文章有四種段落：

- 鬆散性（loose）
- 混合性（mixed）
- 完全性（periodic）
- 循環性（cyclic）

鬆散性段落 Loose paragraph

鬆散性段落（loose paragraph）的主題句（topic sentence）放在段落開首。作者表明主旨（main idea）後，以例子（examples）或解釋（explanations）編寫段落。你正在閱讀的這段落便是一例。

混合性段落 Mixed paragraph

混合性段落（mixed paragraph）的主題句放在段落中間。有時候，要表達段落的中心思想需要先說明才可建立起來，接着，便以例子或解釋闡明之。

完全性段落 Periodic paragraph

完全性段落（periodic paragraph）以主題句結束段落。這方法可讓中心思想根據邏輯逐步建立起來，到最後主題句也因而更易理解，使讀者印象更深。

注意！

完全性段落（periodic paragraph）後接鬆散性段落（loose paragraph）是連結段落的好方法。

循環性段落 Cyclic paragraph

循環性段落（cyclic paragraph）以主題句開首和結束（或以兩種不同方式在段落的開首和結束寫出主題句）。重申中心思想不但可鞏固論點，還可再度提醒讀者，尤其以長段落而言。

撰寫段落 Writing a paragraph

開始 Starting off

要撰寫文章，可先從每段落的主題句（topic sentence）入手。撰寫段落時，要緊記主題句，但這並不表示一定要放主題句在開首。主題句的位置可在段落成形後才決定。

每一個段落也需有其模式或思路，以將其維繫成一個整體。如下例：

敘述段落 Describing paragraph

段落的開首可先作廣泛敘述，然後逐漸轉移焦點至某人或某物上：

The primroses were over. Towards the edge of the wood where the ground became open and sloped down to an old fence and a brambley ditch beyond, only a few fading patches of pale yellow still showed among the dog's mercury and oak-tree roots. On the other side of the fence, the upper part of the field was full of rabbit holes...

—Opening lines of Watership Down
By Richard Adams

報春花已凋謝了。朝着樹林的邊緣，大地變得廣闊無際，沿下傾斜至殘舊

的籬笆，後方是長滿荊棘的溝渠，只剩下幾塊正在枯萎的淡黃花小花圃仍在野藜與橡樹根之間顯而易見。在籬笆的另一邊，田地的上方佈滿了兔子的洞穴⋯⋯

— *Watership Down* 一書的開首
作者：Richard Adams

或可先談焦點，後談周遭環境：

The great fish moved silently through the night water, propelled by short sweeps of its crescent tail. The mouth was open just enough to permit a rush of water over the gills. The land seemed almost as dark as the water, for there was no moon...

—*Opening lines of* Jaws *by Peter Benchley*

巨魚暗暗地在黑夜的海水游動，用新月形的魚尾輕擺前進。牠微張口至足以讓水湧進鰓內。陸地跟海水同樣漆黑一片，因為天上並無月光⋯⋯

— *Jaws* 一書的開首；作者：Peter Benchley

提示

可嘗試就顏色、聲音、氣味等方面統一敍述性的段落（describing paragraph）。

時序段落 Time sequence paragraph

最簡易的模式就是順序。盡量避免如下例般明顯的段落：

I woke up... got out of bed... dressed and had breakfast.
我醒來⋯⋯起床⋯⋯更衣和吃早餐。

以下寫法較有趣：

The wash-basins were in the boys' cloakroom just outside the main hall. I got most of the paint off and as I was drying my hands that's when it happened. I don't know what came over me. As soon as I saw that balaclava lying there on the floor, I decided to pinch it. I couldn't help it. I just knew that this was my only chance. I've never pinched anything before — I don't think I have, but I didn't think of this as... well... I don't even like saying it — but... well stealing. I just did it.

— *From* The Balaclava Story *by George Layton*

洗臉盆就在大堂外的男洗手間內。我洗清大部份顏料，當我在弄乾雙手時，那事就發生了。我不知道我怎麼了。我乍看見那巴拉克拉凡帽倘在地上，就把心一橫要偷去它。我無法自控，只知道那是我唯一一次機會。我從來沒有偷東西──我想是沒有的，但我當時並不認為這行為等同⋯⋯呀⋯⋯我實在不喜歡説出口──呀⋯⋯等同偷竊。我剛剛做了。

──摘錄自 *The Balaclava Story*
作者：George Layton

説明性段落 Explaining paragraph

某些段落用來説明某物的操作或某物的意思。要讓讀者明白當中的説明，有兩件事非做不可：

- 保持顯淺易明！只集中要點，刪除所有無關的文字。

- 確保每一論點或事實能循邏輯發展至下一論點或事實。

含主題段落 Paragraphs with a theme

文章或任何正式文章的段落均需有中心思想，以及説明主題的主題句。選辭、句子結構及使用比喻（figures of speech）的方式都有助闡明主題。

EXTRA Information　見第三章「比喻語言 Figurative language」。

使用連詞 Using connectives

'Connective' also hold other things together!

「連接物」也可連起其他東西。

連詞（connective）連繫句子或段落。

連詞（connective）有助讀者在閱讀時連繫句子的詞彙（word）和短語（phrase）。連詞用於句子與句子之間，使段落得以統一；用於段落與段落之間，使全文流暢。使用連詞的方法如下：

句子與句子之間
Between sentences

- 副詞（adverbs）例如 'although'（「雖然」）、'however'（「但是」）、'therefore'（「因此」）和 'nevertheless'（「然而」）等，可以連結句子：

Some people say the moon is made of green cheese. However, no mice have yet launched an expedition there.

有些人説月亮是用綠奶酪造的，但卻從沒有老鼠登陸月球。

Some people say the moon is made of green cheese. Nevertheless, I think that mature Cheddar is more likely.

有些人説月亮是用綠奶酪造的，然而我認為應是用重切德奶酪所造的才對。

Although some people say the moon is made of green cheese, Neil Armstrong and his pals couldn't even find a bit of rind.

雖然有些人説月亮是用綠奶酪造的，但尼爾岩士唐及其隊友連一丁點奶酪外皮也找不到。

- 我們也可用短語（phrase），如 'for instance'（「例如」）、'for example'（「舉例説」）、'another case'（「另一例子是」）、'on the other hand'（「反過來説」）來連繫句子。

- 時間副詞（adverb of time），如 'then'（「之後」）、'after this'（「然後」）、'meanwhile'（「當時」）、'now'（「現在」）、'consequently'（「最終」）等，也是有用的連詞，但切勿過份使用！

- 連接詞（conjunctions）'and'（「和」）、'but'（「但是」）與 'because'（「因為」）可作句子開首連起段落。

- 雖然在文中重複説話常被視為壞習慣，但刻意重複某詞彙可統一文章並作強調之用：

The other four stared at me in wonder. Then, as the sheer genius of the plot began to sink in, they all started grinning. They slapped me on the back. They cheered me and danced around the classroom. 'We'll do it today!' they cried. 'We'll do it on the way home! YOU had the idea,' they said to me, 'so YOU can be the one to put the mouse in the jar!'

— From *Boy* by *Roald Dahl*

另外四人用驚奇的眼光定睛看着我。接着，當他們發覺妙計天衣無縫時，都開始咧嘴而笑，在我的背上大力拍打一下，振奮我的心情，又在

課室內起舞。「我們今天就去做！」他們喊着說。「我們在回家途中就去做！鬼主意是你想出來的。」他們對我說：「那就由你來放老鼠進瓶子裏！」

—— 摘錄自 *Boy*，作者是 Roald Dahl

段落與段落之間
Between paragraphs

• 以怎樣的主題句結束段落，也可用類似風格的主題句開始下一個段落。

> **EXTRA** *Information* 　見第三章「段落 The paragraph」。

• 適當時可以用副詞短語（adverb phrase）'in the same way...'（「同樣地……」）開始新的段落。

句子變化 Sentence variation

檢查句子長度

檢查句子 (sentence) 長度。

寫好段落的第一稿後,檢查:

- 句子長度 (sentence length):句子長度是否多樣化?每一個段落的句子也應有長有短,有簡單句 (simple sentence),有複合句 (complex sentence)。

- 句子種類 (sentence type):只用鬆散句 (loose sentence) 會使段落乏味無趣。偶爾要運用完全句 (periodic sentence) 或混合句 (mixed sentence),以增添句子種類。

***EXTRA** Information*   見第三章「段落種類 Types of paragraphs」。

More to Learn

寫作過程 The writing process

'What is written without effort is in general read without pleasure.'

「沒用心寫的，一般也讀之無味。」

—Dr Samuel Johnson 森姆莊遜博士（1709–84）

要寫出好文章，一定要作好準備為文章不斷起草稿。利用電腦來做這功夫很容易：先用電腦寫作，細閱每一個段落，需要時便直接修改。不時也應印出稿件來細閱，在稿件上記錄要再用電腦修改的地方。你正在閱讀的這些文字就是這樣寫出來的。

即使是最成功和最富經驗的作者也會細心審閱每一句和每一段，以求達至滿意為止。這就是他們寫作的成功之道！

溫習 Revision

A. 從方框選取正確的連詞來完成文章。

> and   but   Meanwhile   on the other hand   then
>
> After   Therefore   because   However

Sarah didn't know what to do. She had been given a great opportunity

1. _____ the timing was so bad! Her boss wanted her to go on an important business trip the day her best friend was getting married in France! On the one hand, her best friend would be so upset if Sarah didn't go,

2. _____, if she missed the business trip, she would probably lose her job. 3. _____, the decision was extremely tough. She decided to go on a walk to try and clear her head 4. _____ she couldn't make this big decision whilst sitting at her desk.

5. _____ a walk in the park, she didn't feel much better about her situation. She decided that she would first talk to her boss 6. _____ explain the situation to him, 7. _____, she would make her final decision. She hoped that her boss would understand and allow her to miss the business trip.

8. _____, her boss was not the least bit understanding. He was outraged and said that if she went to the wedding, she'd be fired.

9. _____, Sarah's best friend was emailing her to make sure that she was coming to the wedding. She wanted Sarah to be maid of honour.

B. 分辨以下段落屬於「loose」（鬆散性）、「mixed」（混合性）、「periodic」（完全性），還是「cyclic」（循環性）。

Description	Types of Paragraphs
1. A paragraph which explains and develops the topic, then states the topic sentence at the end.	
2. The beginning of the paragraph contains the topic sentence. The rest of the paragraph explains and gives examples of this.	
3. The main point is said at the beginning and at the end.	
4. Examples are given to explain the topic sentence, which is placed in the middle.	

C. 圈出正確連詞來完成句子。

1. (Although / However) people say learning English is easy, I find it very tricky.

2. I don't like eating eggs, (therefore / however) I do like cakes!

3. Sam's piano teacher didn't turn up. His lesson, (therefore / nevertheless) didn't take place.

4. He didn't like running, (although / nevertheless), he completed the charity race and raised a lot of money.

5. (Therefore / Although) Amy worked hard, she still failed her exam.

語言的特別運用 Special uses of language

語體 Register

'Right! Now, first I need to know your correct point of departure.
Then, please enumerate each of the stopping points en route to your
destination...'

「好！首先，我要知道你出發的正確地點。然後，
請列出往目的地途中的每一個停留地點……」

或許他應嘗試用另一種語體（register）。

語體（register）是令語言發揮功用的級別。一位母親跟一個四歲小孩説話會使用甚低級的語體；一名老師跟中學六年級的學生説話會使用較高級的語體；兩名大學教授談論阿仙奴對利物浦的足球比賽時，可能會使用介乎以上兩例級別之間的語體。

語體主要視乎三樣東西：

- 詞彙（vocabulary）
- 句子結構（sentence structure）
- 所用語言在某情景裏面的合適程度（the suitability of language to a situation）

詞彙 Vocabulary

英語中有許多詞彙含相近意思：

start（開始）：*begin*（開始）　　*commence*（開始）　　*found*（成立）
　　　　　　　　originate（源自）

tiny（細小）：　*small*（細小）　　　*little*（細小）　　　*minuscule*（極小）
　　　　　　　　microscopic（微細）

以上某些詞彙很明顯不適合跟小孩或剛學英語的人使用。因此，'There's only a tiny drop at the bottom of the glass'（「玻璃杯杯底只剩下一小水滴而已」）的語體較 'A microscopic quantity of liquid remains in the flask'（「玻璃瓶剩餘微小份量的液體」）的語體為低級。

注意！

較低級的語體不等於「錯」。跟小孩子説話時所用的語言，會比跟教授説話時所用的較簡易。

所用的詞彙應適合：

- 説話對象
- 談論的話題
- 説話者身處的情景

句子結構 Sentence structure

運用詞彙須隨着情景而變化，所以句子中所用的詞彙可能只適用於某些人物、話題和情景，卻不適用於其他情況。

簡單句子（simple sentence）可使語體處於低級，故説話者要根據「聽眾」來改變句子模式（sentence pattern）。見下例：

(1) *I have a cat. It has two eyes. They are green. They change in different lights. Cats are quite marvellous creatures!*

　　我有一隻貓。牠有兩隻眼睛。雙眼是綠色的。牠們會隨着不同燈光轉變。貓真是不可思議的生物！

(2) *My cat's two green eyes change when the light changes. This is one of the reasons why cats are such marvellous creatures.*

　　我的貓的一雙綠眼睛會隨着不同燈光轉變。這是其中一個原因可解釋貓為何是不可思議的生物。

例句（2）的句式比例句（1）更加複合（complex），語體（register）也比例句（1）高級。更高級的語體如下例：

(3) *The green eyes of cats adapt marvellously to varying intensities of light.*

　　貓的綠眼睛能不可思議地適應不同的光度。

所用語言在某情景中的合適程度
The suitability of language to a situation

良好的溝通，就如照相機的腳架般，倚靠着三腳支撐——內容（content）、聽眾（audience）和動機（motivation）——英語縮寫為 CAM。要在説話或寫作中溝通良好，就要常緊記 CAM。以下幾點必要知道：

- What——説話者在説甚麼（內容）
- Who——説話者的説話對象是誰（聽眾）
- Why——説話者為甚麼説話（動機）

甚麼？——內容
What? — The content

説話者想説甚麼會決定他／她怎樣説。例如，數字和統計數據最好不説出來；生日願望最好不是打出來的（生日願望屬私人性質，應手寫出來）；年終報告不應大聲讀出，而是供印製出來閱讀的。

<hr>

注意！

查一查怎樣表達想説的話才是最佳方法——是透過説話還是寫字？圖表（diagram）、圖解（chart）和相片（photograph）是否有幫助？

<hr>

誰人？——聽眾
Who? — The audience

表達意思的方式有許多種類，運用哪一種要視乎説話對象。跟朋友聊天與跟主任面試會有很大分別！在課堂上站出來跟全班同學説話也有別於在學校集會上站出來跟全校同學説話。

同樣，聽眾也可能有男有女、有老有少——甚至會有英語能力不佳的。

> **注意！**
>
> 每當説話或寫作之前，要先考慮説話對象。

為甚麼？——目的
Why? — The purpose

説話的原因會影響溝通方法。用來説服人所説或所寫的語體（register）和語氣（tone），就跟警告人、教導人或逗人發笑的不同。

> **注意！**
>
> 要確保説話語氣（tone）跟目的（purpose）配合。

若包含「內容、聽眾、動機」的「CAM 三腳架」中，其中一隻腳倒下，整個結構也會倒下，所以要小心考慮 'What（甚麼）？'、'Why（為何）？' 和 'Whom（誰人）？' 等問題，弄清楚三者！

標準英語 Standard English

'Luv a duck. Then the ol'girl...
she fell darn the apples 'n' pears'.
「哎呀！接着那年老的女士從樓梯跌了下來。」

標準英語（Standard English）是一個所有人也能明白的方言（dialect）。

標準英語（standard English）是「正式」英語（'official' English）的名稱 ── 遵守字典（dictionary）和語法書（grammar book）規則的一套英語，亦即在商業書信（business letter）和正式文章中運用的英語，同時也是大部份電視新聞記者的用語。

標準英語並不是唯一的一種「正確」英語。其他常見的種類，如地區方言（regional dialects）也是恰當及有價值的。畢竟人類遠早在語法書籍面世前已能成功説英語。

再者，語言常變，而英語的規則也非牢不可改。昨日的「錯誤」也可能會收錄在明天的語法書中！

然而，標準英語作為「通行貨幣」是很有用的，即使我們不是都説標準英語，但我們都能理解它，因此所有人在學校裏也學標準英語。

非正式語言 Informal language

慣用語 Idioms

慣用語（idioms）是在特定語言中具特別意義的短語（phrases），外地人常覺得這些慣用語難以理解或翻譯。'idiom' 源自相同希臘詞根 'idiot'，意謂私人的、獨有的、只屬於一人的東西。

例如，若對法國人說 'Use your loaf and get cracking!'（「動動腦筋，開始做事！」）的話，他必感大惑不解。他想：'Where's the bread?'（「麵包在哪裏？」）'What do I crack with it?'（「用它來弄破甚麼？」）

More to Learn

以下慣用語是甚麼意思？
What do these idioms mean?

1. You've put your foot in it.
2. Keep your hair on!
3. Hard cheese!
4. A chip off the old block
5. Don't fly off the handle.
6. It's a breeze.
7. You're in hot water!
8. To send to Coventry
9. To put two and two together

答案：
1. 你作了得罪別人的事 / 説了得罪別人的話
2. 保持冷靜
3. 惡運
4. 跟父母相似的人，尤指性格方面
5. 別無故發脾氣
6. 容易的工作
7. 你有麻煩
8. 拒絕與某人談話 / 拒絕理睬某人
9. 根據所見所聞來推測真相

你可以想出其他使人絞盡腦汁的慣用語嗎？

注意！

語言常變，慣用語經常由人創造出來。

陳腔濫調 Cliché

陳腔濫調（cliché）是陳腐過時的用語，現已失去震撼力與新鮮感，但電視和電台仍不時使用。可嘗試找出它們，但切勿運用！以下提供了一些例子：

first and foremost（首要）；*at the end of the day*（從各方面看）；*over the moon*（狂喜）；*sick as a parrot*（對某事感到很失望）；*I hear what you're saying*（我明白你的意思）；*peace and quiet*（和平寧靜）；*last but not least*（最後但也同樣重要的）；*raining cats and dogs*（傾盆大雨）；*hard as nails*（鐵石心腸）；*the blushing bride*（羞赧的新娘）；*to make or break*（成敗的關鍵）

陳詞濫調（cliché）是法語中模子（mould）的意思。模子（mould）是常造出相同形狀東西的物件。

俚語 Slang

俚語（slang）是日常生活中仍不視作禮貌或不為正式對話所接受的詞彙和短語。俚語不會用於正式文章（除了記錄對話，或製造特別效果，如幽默感之外）。

俚語有四種：

• 舊詞新義：

例子（舊詞）	意思（新義）
dough（生麵團） *bread*（麵包） *readies*（現金）	*money*（金錢）
anorak（防水有帽外套）	*a total enthusiast with no other interests*（只對某一事物鍾情的狂熱者）

• 沒被正式接受使用的外來詞彙（foreign words）：

例子	來源	意思
vamoose	墨西哥語 '*vamos*'	*let us go*（讓我們走）
pronto	西班牙語「立刻」的意思	*immediately, very soon*（立即，很快）

• 新造詞彙（newly coined words）：

例子	意思
ginormous	*gigantic*（龐大）+ *enormous*（巨大）
nimbyism	*a resistance to new building, etc.*（「對新建築物的抗拒」等等）（源自 *Not In My Back Yard*）

• 取替其他詞彙或短語的詞彙和短語：

例子	意思
butcher's（屠夫的）	*look*（看）（倫敦土話的同韻俚語：*butcher's hook*［屠夫的鉤子］）
the big smoke（巨大煙霧）	*city*（城市）

More to Learn

同韻俚語：以下句子是甚麼意思？

Rhyming slang: what do these mean?

Climb the apples and pears
   = climb the stairs（爬樓梯）

Let's scarper.（源自 *'Scapa Flow'*）
   = let's go.（一起走吧。）

My plates are aching!（源自 *'plates of meat'*）
   = my feet are aching!（我雙腳疼痛！）

Do you fancy a ball or chalk?
   = do you fancy a walk?（你想散步嗎？）

Would you Adam and Eve it?
   = would you believe it?（你會相信嗎？）

Give us a butcher's.（源自 *'butcher's hook'*）
   = give us a look.（望一望我們。）

Across the frog and toad
   = across the road（走過道路）

俚語（slang）雖不可用在正式對話或文章中，但這並不等於要否定它。俚語可為語言注入新生命。此外，俚語詞彙是可逐漸得到認同的。例如，'donkey'（「驢」），（源自 dun，即暗褐色 [light brown] + -ke 即表示親切的後綴 [affectionate suffix]），在一個世紀以前曾是俚語。

口語用語 Colloquialism

口語短語（colloquial phrase）相等於俚語用語（slang expression），為多數人所熟識。除最正式的對話外，在所有對話中也得以運用。口語用語（colloquialism）同時也可以是慣用語（idiom）。

He gave the driver a dirty look.
他以厭惡的眼神看着司機。

How ghastly! 糟透了！

She was bumped off. 她遭謀殺。

Are you with it? 你有潮流觸覺嗎？

然而，口語用語一般都不在正式文章裏採用。要寫文章，就要另覓正式用語。

術語 Jargon

術語（jargon）指某行業、專業或排外的羣體（exclusive group）使用的特有詞彙和短語。對外界人來説，術語並不容易理解：

以印刷行業的術語而言，*'put to bed'* 指安排已全審閱過的報紙最終版本付印，準備「印製」（*'run'*）。

在滑浪的術語中，*'wipe out'* 解作倒下或傾覆。

在音樂界的術語中，*'middle eight'* 指標準流行曲中樂器的中間部份（共八音節長）。

在管理階層的術語中，*'cascading'* 指訓練或提供資料給某些人，而他們必定要將之傳授給其他人。

術語，如專有名詞般，是「速記法」（*'shorthand'*）的一種，可以簡化説話內容。

切勿對不明白術語（jargon）的人使用術語。

比喻 Figure of speech

‘Porky! Your room is a pigsty.’
「豬仔！你的房間簡直是個豬舍。」

當然只是比喻（figure of speech）而已。

比喻（figure of speech）即任何非依照字面本義解釋的詞彙（word）或短語（phrase），又或是慣用語（idiom）。也就是説，這些詞彙或短語的意思並非字面上的意思。例如，‘it's raining cats and dogs’ 並不是説每當陰雲密佈時也要小心會有貓狗從天上掉下來；‘your bedroom is a pigsty’ 也非説衣櫃裏會有小豬走出來。使用比喻的最常見方法有三種：

比喻語言 Figurative language

包括日常生活中用作比喻的詞彙：

the hands of a clock 時鐘上的時針秒針

the foot of a mountain 山腳

saying someone is big-headed 說某人自命不凡

明喻 Simile

明喻（simile）指直接比較兩種有共同特點的物件。詞彙如 'like'（「好像」）或 'as'（「如」）可用作指出比較：

as slippery as an eel 如鰻魚般滑

My father-in-law had a face like a bag of spanners.

我岳父的臉瘦削如一個盛着板手的袋子。

Grammar Clinic

有許多明喻（similes）已變成陳腔濫調（clichés）

EXTRA Information 見第三章「非正式語言 Informal language」。

as good as gold 如金般好（= 表現很好）
as heavy as lead 如鉛般重（= 很重）
as pretty as a picture 如畫般美（= 非常漂亮）……

自己構想出明喻會更有個人風格，也更為有趣：

as cold as a fridge in winter 如冬季的冰箱般寒冷
as hard as my Granny's rock cakes
如祖母的石頭蛋糕般硬
skin like a spotwelder's bench
如點焊工人工作桌般的皮膚

暗喻 Metaphor

如明喻（simile）般，暗喻（metaphor）比較兩件物件，但更為直接，而且不使用 'like'（「好像」）或 'as'（「如」）的詞彙。

'metaphor' 源自希臘詞彙，指「轉送」、「轉移」：

Arnie was a man-mountain 阿里是一個人造山峯

the striker was a goal machine 那擊球手是個入球機器

the shop was a little gold mine 那店鋪是個金礦

暗喻很常用，一般也在不知不覺中使用了：

the key to a problem 問題的關鍵

a car ploughs into a bus queue
一輛汽車撞入一些正在排隊等巴士的人

your brother makes a pig of himself 你弟弟吃得太多

注意！

切勿混合暗喻，否則效果會強差人意或變得荒謬：

- ✗ We must put our best foot forward, take the bull by the horns and leave no stone unturned.

  我們必定要從速行事，勇敢地面對困難，以及絞盡腦汁。

- ✗ He grasped the nettle while it was hot.

  他在問題棘手時堅定果斷地處理了。

特別效果 Special effects

Antithesis（對偶）　　**alliteration**（頭韻）　　**pun**（雙關語）
euphemism（委婉語）　**onomatopoeia**（擬聲詞）　**irony**（反語）
assonance（半諧語）　**proverb**（諺語）　**sarcasm**（諷刺）　**innuendo**（影射）

嘗試運用特別的寫作技巧（writing technique）。

有許多特別技巧（special technqiue）可使文章更有趣或令人留下深刻印象。這些技巧能否發揮效用，要視乎是否在適當時候和位置使用，這方面是需要練習的。下例作出示範：

頭韻 Alliteration

頭韻（alliteration）指重複使用開首字母（通常是用輔音 [consonant]）或聲音來製造效果。這方法可使讀者更容易記着某短語。許多書名和廣告也用頭韻：

Charlie and the Chocolate Factory《查理與巧克力工廠》

Pride and Prejudice《傲慢與偏見》

Dumb and Dumber《絕世孖寶》

詩篇（poems）中也有不少例子：

the forest's ferny floor
森林中長滿蕨類植物的地面

the stuttering rifle's rapid rattle
口吃步槍的快速格格響聲

When fishes flew and forests walked
當魚兒浮游與森林行走時

對偶 Antithesis

對偶（antithesis）放兩個相反的主意於一句內，以帶出兩者之間的對比：

The wisest fool in Christendom (said about King James I).
世上所有基督教國家中最聰明的傻瓜（談論詹姆士王一世）。

No, madam, Bach is not composing; he is decomposing.
錯了，太太，巴哈不是在創作，而是在腐爛。

半諧音 Assonance

半諧音（assonance）是兩個或以上的字之間的元音（vowels）押韻（輔音 [consonants] 不押韻）。押韻詞彙的相隔距離必須足以製造效果。試讀出以下短語，聽出重複的元音：

Better than voices of winds that sing

比懂歌唱的風聲更美好

Silence and emptiness with dark stars passing

有黑暗星星越過的寂靜與空虛

Deep Heat

暗藏的強烈感情

委婉語 Euphemism

委婉語（euphemism）是間接或刻意婉轉的方法，來指出一些令人不快的事情：

意思	委婉語
death（死亡）	*passing away*、*passing on* 或 *falling asleep*
murder（謀殺）	*bumping off*、*rubbing out* 或 *a hit*
the lavatory（洗手間）	*bathroom*、*cloakroom* 或 *little girls' room*

影射 Innuendo

影射（innuendo）透過提示或暗示表達意思，常因要說一些令人不快的話而使用：

That new gold watch you are wearing is remarkably like the one I lost last month!

你戴着的新買金製手錶跟我在上月遺失的手錶非常相似！

反語 Irony

反語（irony）即説話跟意思相反（opposite），通常可從説話者的語氣清楚得知：

Teacher to dozy, inattentive class: 'You're a really bright lot this afternoon!'

教師對昏昏欲睡、毫不留心的學生説：「這個下午你們真是一羣聰明伶俐的人！」

More to Learn

諷刺 Sarcasm

諷刺的説話（sarcastic remarks）是反語（irony）的殘酷版本。例如，惡霸絆倒一名小孩之後説：「噢！查理跌倒弄傷自己了！」（'Oh dear! Charlie's fallen and hurt himself!'）

'sarcasm' 源自希臘文，指 'to tear at like a dog'（「如撕開狗一樣」）。

擬聲詞 Onomatopoeia

擬聲詞（onomatopoeia）運用跟描述聲音相似的詞彙：

splash（撲通一聲的濺潑聲）　*squelch*（咯吱咯吱聲）　*buzz*（嗡嗡聲）
pitter-patter（劈啪聲）　*zoom*（快速移動的嗡嗡聲）

諺語 Proverb

諺語（proverb）教導人生哲理，是一些普及的簡短格言：

A stitch in time saves nine.
及時行動可為日後省掉額外工夫。

Beggars can't be choosers.
饑不擇食。

溫習 Revision

A. 分辨以下各短語屬於「simile」(明喻) 還是「metaphor」(暗喻)。

1. as cold as ice _____

2. a blanket of snow _____

3. I slept like a log. _____

4. as bright as a button _____

5. jumping for joy _____

6. You smell like a rose. _____

7. She is the apple of my eye! _____

8. He ate like a pig. _____

9. She had a broken heart. _____

10. Her legs are as long as a giraffes. _____

B. 以下各句使用了甚麼特別效果？在橫線上填上「alliteration」(頭韻)、
「onomatopoeia」(擬聲詞)，還是「proverb」(諺語)。

1. The fish fed on fruit and bread. _____

2. The mud squelched under her feet. _____

3. The gorgeous, green jacket looked beautiful on her. _____

4. 'A friend in need is a friend indeed,' said Jim's mum. _____

5. It's harsh, but true, beggars can't be choosers! _____

6. He slammed the door behind him. _____

7. His speech was big, bold and brilliant. _____

8. The lorry crashed into the lamppost. _____

9. Hong Kong is hot, humid and horrible in the summer. _____

C. 分辨以下各句的語體屬於「high register」(高級) 還是「low register」(低級)。

1. The cat ate his food. _____

2. The miniature creature perched on the rock. _____

3. An obscure butterfly fluttered through the window. _____

4. My homework is boring and hard. _____

5. My old, stupid phone ran out of battery. _____

6. The spectacular sunshine is beating down upon the earth. _____

7. A big spider came into my room and made a web. _____

D. 以下各句使用了甚麼類型的非正式語言？在表格內填上「idiom」(慣用語)、「cliché」(陳腔濫調) 或「slang」(俚語)。

1. He was over the moon.	
2. She managed to kill two birds with one stone.	
3. It was a mega party.	
4. At the end of the day, it wasn't my fault.	
5. The exam was a piece of cake.	
6. He put two and two together and understood why she was acting strange.	
7. She thought that he was absolute scum.	

附錄 Appendices

答案 Answer Key

漢英索引 Chinese-English Index

英漢索引 English-Chinese Index

温習好幫手 Revision Card

答案 Answer Key

第一章 詞彙 Parts of speech

A 詞類 Parts of speech

A. (p.51)

1. What's
2. My
3. Somebody
4. I
5. their
6. that
7. whose
8. myself
9. She

B. (p.51)

1. extremely
2. some
3. slowly
4. fish
5. wolves
6. angry
7. the
8. soon
9. those
10. orange
11. bus
12. an
13. mosquitoes
14. a
15. Because of

C. (p.52)

1. took
2. was
3. went
4. going
5. is
6. are
7. doing
8. finish
9. started

D. (p.52)

1. long holiday
2. large bag
3. strong wind
4. adorable puppy
5. several people
6. interesting book
7. difficult exam

E. (p.53)

1. and
2. under
3. over
4. up
5. after
6. but
7. so
8. behind
9. While
10. as
11. from

F. (p.53)

1. My
2. went
3. She
4. few
5. a
6. x
7. beautiful
8. and
9. amazingly
10. at
11. theirs

G. (p.54)

1. Who broke his arm?
2. Where is Frank going today?
3. Who did she shout at?
4. Why did they have to go inside?
5. How many people came to the show?
6. What did she buy?
7. How did the man run?
8. When is he arriving?

B 造詞 Word building

A. (p.63)

1. goodness
2. treatment
3. forgetful
4. billionaire
5. childish
6. admit
7. antiviolence
8. semicolon
9. distasteful
10. unappealing

B. (p.63)

1. preview
2. watching
3. enjoyable
4. misunderstood
5. disliked

C. (p.64)

1. B – Buyer
2. D – Excitement
3. A – Fixable

4.   C – Hopeless

D.   (p.64)

1.	outside	2.	sports-mad
3.	basketball	4.	well-known
5.	ice-skating	6.	action-packed

C 拼寫指南 Spelling guide

A.   (p.72)

1.	stories	2.	lying
3.	paid	4.	berries
5.	cities		

B.   (p.72)

1.   accommodation
2.   argument
3.   calendar
4.   independent
5.   occurrence
6.   experience

C.   (p.73)

1.	shopping	2.	hoping
3.	dinner	4.	disappointing
5.	excellent	6.	dessert
7.	putting		

D.   (p.73)

1.   begining (beginning)
2.   dificult (difficult)
3.   foriegn (foreign)
4.   jelous (jealous)
5.   hieght (height)
6.   though (through)
7.   priveleged (privileged)
8.   gratful (grateful)
9.   recieved (received)
10.   achievment (achievement)

E.   (p.73)

1.	i) heavier	2.	ii) skiing
3.	i) panicking	4.	i) really
5.	i) weird	6.	i) piece
7.	i) commitment	8.	i) achieve

D 使用字典 Using a dictionary

A.   (p.82)

1.	animal	2.	horse
3.	insect	4.	interesting
5.	money	6.	monkey
7.	name	8.	normal
9.	yacht	10.	zebra

B.   (p.82)

1.	phrase	2.	noun
3.	verb	4.	verb
5.	noun		

C.   (p.83)

1.	D	2.	A
3.	F	4.	G
5.	C	6.	E
7.	B		

D.   (p.83)

1.	False	2.	True
3.	False	4.	True

E 同義詞與反義詞 Synonyms and antonyms

A.   (p.86)

1.	synonyms	2.	synonyms
3.	antonym	4.	antonym
5.	synonym	6.	antonym
7.	synonym	8.	antonym
9.	synonym	10.	antonym

B.   (p.86)

1.	impossible	2.	uninterested
3.	impolite	4.	informal

5. invisible   6. unnecessary

C. (p.87)

1. im   2. un
3. im   4. im
5. un   6. un
7. dis   8. in

D. (p.87)

1. priceless
2. endless
3. colourless
4. pointless
5. harmless

第二章 詞組與句子
Word Groups and the Sentence

A 句子 The sentence

A. (p.108)

1. The pen is on the table.
2. He ate an apple.
3. She went to the zoo.
4. The talk was interesting.
5. The food was delicious.
6. Fruit is good for you.
7. The black dress was very expensive.
8. Their holiday was fantastic.

B. (p.108)

1. object   2. subject
3. object   4. verb
5. verb   6. subject

C. (p.109)

1. Was the water cold?
2. Was the ice-cream delicious?
3. Have you been to Thailand?
4. Have you seen the new school building?

5. Has he finished his homework?
6. Are the people friendly?

D. (p.109)

1. verb   2. noun
3. noun   4. noun
5. verb   6. adjective

E. (p.109)

1. where I was   2. she is
3. what they say   4. who was ill
5. who is   6. Before
7. After   8. because
9. If

F. (p.110)

1. statement   2. question
3. exclamation   4. command
5. wish   6. exclamation
7. wish   8. command
9. question

G. (p.110)

1. Tom fell over and hurt his knee.
2. Emma went to the market and bought some vegetables.
3. Lynn likes apples but she doesn't like bananas.
4. She went to sleep because she was tired.
5. He has been to Thailand but he hasn't been to Cambodia.

B 標點符號 Punctuation

A. (p.129)

1. ?   2. !
3. !   4. ,
5. … / .   6.   —— / ,,

B. (p.129)

1.	'	2.	in case
3.	.	4.	,
5.	Did	6.	,
7.	replied	8.	—

C. (p.130)

1.	:	2.	( )
3.	— —	4.	:
5.	;	6.	*blank*
7.	—	8.	:
9.	( )	10.	; ; ;

D. (p.130)

1.	woman's	2.	7 a.m.
3.	won't	4.	un-British
5.	week's, I'll		

第三章 進階寫作技巧
Advanced Writing Skills

A 段落 The paragraph

A. (p.142)
1. but
2. on the other hand
3. Therefore
4. because
5. After
6. and
7. then
8. However
9. Meanwhile

B. (p.143)

1.	periodic	2.	loose
3.	cyclic	4.	mixed

C. (p.143)

1.	Although	2.	however
3.	therefore	4.	nevertheless

5. although

B 語言的特別運用
Special uses of language

A. (p.163)

1.	simile	2.	metaphor
3.	simile	4.	simile
5.	metaphor	6.	simile
7.	metaphor	8.	simile
9.	metaphor	10.	simile

B. (p.163)
1. alliteration
2. onomatopoeia
3. alliteration
4. proverb
5. proverb
6. onomatopoeia
7. alliteration
8. onomatopoeia
9. alliteration

C. (p.164)

1.	low register	2.	high register
3.	high register	4.	low register
5.	low register	6.	high register
7.	low register		

D. (p.164)

1.	cliché / Idiom	2.	idiom
3.	slang	4.	cliché
5.	idiom	6.	idiom
7.	slang		

漢英 索引
Chinese-English Index

本索引列出語法術語主要出現的頁碼，個別
出現時不詳列。

英漢 索引
English-Chinese Index

本索引列出語法術語主要出現的頁碼，個別
出現時不詳列。

溫習好幫手 Revision Card

此組溫習卡可供讀者剪出來，隨身攜帶，隨時溫習。

如有需要，讀者可以仿效這個做法，按己所需，分主題製作溫習卡自用。

詞類 Parts of speech

造詞 Word building

拼寫指南 Spelling guide

使用字典 Using a dictionary

同義詞與反義詞 Synonyms and antonyms

句子 The sentence

標點符號 Punctuation

段落 The paragraph

語言的特別運用 Special uses of language

名詞 Nouns

名詞（nouns）一般解作名稱。名詞可包括人、地、物件、羣組、質素及觀點的名稱。

- proper 專有
- collective 集體
- common 普通
- abstract 抽象

代詞 Pronouns

代詞（pronoun）是用來代替名詞（noun）的詞彙。代詞可造成以下句子。

Mrs Jones told <u>her</u> son Ron to take <u>his</u> bike out of <u>her</u> car.
鍾斯太太叫兒子朗從她的車裏拿他的腳踏車出來。

以替代如下例般的累贅句子：

Mrs Jones told <u>Mrs Jones's</u> son Ron to take <u>Ron's</u> bike out of <u>Mrs Jones's</u> car.
鍾斯太太叫鍾斯太太的兒子朗從鍾斯太太的車裏拿朗的腳踏車出來。

代詞有七類，分為：

- 人稱（personal）
- 物主（possessive）
- 反身（reflexive）
- 指示（demonstrative）
- 疑問（interrogative）
- 關係（relative）
- 不定（indefinite）

動詞 Verbs

動詞（verbs）是最重要的詞彙，是每個句子必要有的。
動詞說明的東西有二：

- 名詞（noun），或代詞（pronoun）的動作：
  The door <u>opened</u>. 門打開了。
- 名詞（noun），或代詞（pronoun）的動作：
  He <u>is</u> so upset. 他現在很失落。

形容詞 Adjectives

形容詞（adjectives）是為名詞（nouns）或代詞（pronouns）提供更多資料的詞彙。
形容詞常緊置於所描述之詞彙前：

a <u>lively</u> game show 一個生動的運動節目
形容詞（adjectives）有六種主要類別：

- 描述（descriptive）
- 指示（demonstrative）
- 物主（possessive）
- 疑問（interrogative）
- 數字（numerical）
- 數量（quantitative）

副詞 Adverbs

副詞（**adverbs**）道出更多有關動詞（**verbs**），或有時關於形容詞（**adjectives**）的資料。副詞常放在最近動詞的位置，以及在其他詞類（**parts of speech**）之前：

He drove <u>dangerously</u>. 他危險駕駛。

副詞有七種類別：

- 方式（**manner**）
- 時間（**time**）
- 次數（**number**）
- 否定（**negation**）
- 地點（**place**）
- 原因（**reason**）
- 程度（**degree**）

介詞 Prepositions

介詞（**preposition**）是連起兩個名詞（或代詞）的詞彙。

The train went <u>through</u> the tunnel. 火車駛過隧道。

在以上的句子中，**'through'** 展示如何連起 **'train'**（「火車」）和（「隧道」）。

介詞必須放在兩個連結的名詞（或代詞）之間，並緊置於第二個名詞之前：

He dropped the banana <u>from</u> the window.

他從窗戶掉下香蕉。

連接詞 Conjunctions

連接詞（**conjunctions**）是連起句子不同部份的詞彙。

主要的連接詞有：

And（和）	because（因為）	but（但是）
for（為）	however（然而）	since（自從）
until（直至）	yet（但是）	

連接詞（**conjunctions**）有四種類別：

- 並列（**co-ordinating**）
- 相關聯（**co-relative**）
- 對比（**contrasting**）
- 從屬（**subordinating**）

感歎句 Interjections

感歎句（**interjections**）一般是單獨使用的詞彙，常用來表達強烈的感情：

oh（噢）! *phew*（啊）! *drat*（討厭）! *yippee*（妙極）! *hurrah*（好啊）! *hello*（喂）!

辨別詞類——用疑問方法
Spotting parts of speech — the question method

名詞和代詞 Nouns and pronouns

要辨認名詞（noun）和代詞（pronoun），可提問 'What（甚麼）?'、'Who（誰人，作主語用）?' 或 'Whom（誰人，作賓語用）?'

動詞 Verbs

要辨認動詞（verbs），可提問 'What does [or did] the subject do（主語做［或做過］甚麼）?

形容詞 Adjectives

要辨認形容詞（adjective），可提問 'Which（哪些）?'、'What kind of（怎麼樣的）?'、'How many（多少）?'

副詞 Adverbs

要辨認副詞（adverb），可提問 'How（怎樣）'、'Where（哪裏）'、'When（何時）' 或 'Why（為甚麼）?'

介詞 Prepositions

要辨認介詞（prepositions），可在句中找出多個名詞（noun）或代詞（pronoun），然後查看它們是否連結在一起。接着，找出連起它們的詞彙。

詞綴（前綴和後綴）
Affixes (Prefixes and Suffixes)

詞根（root）意指基本詞彙，藉着它可造成其他詞彙（words）。例如，詞根 'cover'（「隱藏」）可變成 uncover（揭露）、discover（發現）、recover（復原）、covering（遮蓋物）、rediscovery（重新發現）等等。

詞彙中新的零碎部份 un-、dis-、-ing 等稱為「詞綴（affixes）」。詞綴有兩個種類：

前綴（prefixes）　　　後綴（suffixes）

前綴（prefix）是一組有特定意思的字母，放在詞根（root）的前面：

tele-vision（電影）、anti-septic（消毒劑）、geo-graphy（地理）

後綴（suffix）是一組有特定功能的字母，放在詞根（root）的後面：

good-ness（善良）、million-aire（百萬富翁）、disturb-ance（騷亂）

派生詞 Derivatives

派生詞（derivatives）是指一個由加上前綴（prefix），有時再加上後綴（suffix），所造出來的新詞。

複合詞 Compounds

由兩個或以上詞彙（words）組合而成的新詞彙稱為複合詞（compounds）。複合詞中的連字符號（hyphens）則是可有可無的。

三個加強拼寫能力的提示
Three hints for better spelling

1. 口齒不清造成差勁的拼寫能力。要改善拼寫能力，在腦海中也要咬字清晰。字典通常會教授正確的發音方法。

2. 大部份拼寫方法奇異的詞彙都是來自其他語言的：
   'Suede'（發音為 swayed）意謂絨面皮，源自法文 'suéde'，即指這類衣物的原產地——瑞典。

3. 訓練自己「拍照」，記下一些有拼寫困難的詞彙，在腦海中把它們組成一幅清晰的照片。還要勇於發明一些幫助自己記憶的方法，例如：Parallel（平行線）一詞中間有兩條平行線。

字典（dictionary）不只記載詞彙的拼寫方法和意思。詞彙按字母的先後次序（alphabetical order）排列。在一本優質字典裏，可找到：

- 中心句（headword）
- 複數（plural）
- 詞類（part of speech）
- 定義（definition）
- 詞源（origin）
- 複合詞（compounds）和派生詞（derivatives）
- 形容詞和副詞的比較級（comparative）與最高級（superlative）
- 短語（phrases）和慣用語（idioms）

成年人使用的字典還提供發音方法（pronunciations）。

同義詞與反義詞 Synonyms and antonyms

同義詞（synonym）意謂具有相同意思的詞彙。

反義詞（antonym）意謂具有相反意思的詞彙。

詞序 Word order

正常的詞序（normal word order）是：主語（subject）─ 動詞（verb）─ 賓語（object）。若改變正常詞序，即主語（Subject）─ 動詞（Verb）─ 賓語（Object），意思也會隨之改變。最常見的改變是變成動詞（Verb）─ 主語（Subject）─ 賓語（Object），以製造疑問句（question）。

短語 Phrases

短語（phrase）是指在句子中可作詞類（part of speech）使用的詞彙組合（group of words）。

分句 Clauses

含有動詞（verb）的短語（phrase）就稱為分句（clause）。分句構成句子（sentences）的部份。

分句主要有三個種類：

- 名詞分句（noun clauses）
- 形容詞分句（adjective clauses）
- 副詞分句（adverb clauses）

句子的種類 Types of sentence

句子有五種：

- 陳述句（statements）
- 疑問句（questions）
- 命令句（commands）
- 感歎句（exclamations）
- 祝願句（wishes）

造句 The construction of sentences

簡單句 Simple sentences

可獨立理解，只含一個動詞而已，並非全是短句！

Most dogs are friendly.
大部份狗兒都很友善。

並列句 Compound sentences

運用連接詞（conjunction），如 'and'（「和」）、'but'（「但是」）、'because'（「因為」）等等；或合適的標點符號（punctuation），組合兩個或以上的簡單句（simple sentences）所構成的句子：

Jack fell down and broke his crown.
傑克跌倒並弄穿了頭。

複合句 Complex sentences

由單一分句加上一個或以上的名詞分句（noun clauses）、形容詞分句（adjective clauses）或副詞分句（adverb clauses）組成：

You ought to be on TV, so we could turn you off!
你應該在電視上出現，那麼我們便可關掉你！

標點符號 Punctuation

結束句子 Ending a sentence

- 句號／腳點（full stop）：(.)
- 問號（question mark）：(?)
- 感歎號（exclamation mark）：(!)
- 直接引語（direct speech）：(' 或 ")

    She said nervously, 'I'm just a harmless pupil. Why are you confusing me with all this grammar?
    她緊張地說：「我只是一個無辜的學生。為甚麼你要用這些語法來為難我？」

- 破折號（dash）：(—)

    'The cabin's on fire and the ship's going to—' Abruptly, the commander's voice ceased. A deathly silence spread over Mission Control.
    「船艙？火了，船也將——」突然間，船長不作聲。一片寂靜蔓延至整個指揮部。

- 省略號（dots）：(...)

    Between us we swung the body of the murdered crook far out into the river. The evil eyes of an alligator glinted greedily...
    我們兩人合力拋那遭謀殺的騙子屍體進河中。鱷魚邪惡的眼睛貪婪地閃亮着……

段落 The paragraph

段落（paragraph）即指與某題目相關的一組句子。在正式的文章中，段落中的每一句句子（sentence）也必須跟這個主旨（main idea）相關。

主題句 The topic sentence

為文章編寫段落，每一段落也應有「主題句」（'topic sentence'），以清楚表明段落的中心思想。主題句通常是段落的開首句子，但這並不是規定的。故事（stories）或敘述文（narrative）的段落則不一定需要主題句。

段落種類 Types of paragraph

文章有四種段落：

- 鬆散性（loose）
- 混合性（mixed）
- 完全性（periodic）
- 循環性（cyclic）

語體 Register

語體（register）是令語言發揮功用的級別。一位母親跟一個四歲小孩說話會使用甚低級的語體；一名老師跟中學六年級的學生說話會使用較高級的語體；兩名大學教授談論阿仙奴對利物浦的足球比賽時，可能會使用介乎以上兩例級別之間的語體。

語體主要視乎三樣東西：

- 語彙（vocabulary）
- 句子結構（sentence structure）
- 所有語言在某情景中的合適程度（the suitability of language to a situation）

句子中的標點符號 Punctuation within sentences

逗號（The comma）：（ , ）

逗號（commas）用在讀者需停頓的位置。下列情況必要使用逗號：

- 在清單（list）中分開詞彙（words）和短語（phrases）：
- 在句子（sentence）中分開詞彙和短語：
- 在句子中分開分句（clauses）：

He added, while my face turned a shade of purple, that I was a fool.
當我臉色發紫時，他還說我是個蠢才。

- 以名字稱呼說話對象時
- 使用修整句子的副詞（adverbs）和副詞短語（adverb phrases）時（詞彙如however [但是]、nevertheless [然而]、therefore [因此]、of course [當然]、in fact [事實上]、for instance [例如] 等等）：
- 在直接引語（direct speech）中：

'OK,' he muttered, 'you can have your money back.'
「好，」他咕嚕地說：「你可取回退款。」

句子中的標點符號 Punctuation within sentences

分號（The semi-colon）：（；）

分號（semi-colon）現在比以前較少用，但它卻很有用。下列情況可使用分號：

- 不使用連接詞（conjunction）連起兩句或以上的簡單句子（simple sentences）。只有當第二句子與第一句子之間存在着很強的連繫時才可使用分號
- 當一連串的從句（subordinate clauses）皆以同一動詞（verb）連繫時
- 當清單中的獨立項目已需用上逗號時，便要使用分號分隔開項目
- 當在平衡的句子（balanced sentences）中，兩句分句使用同一動詞，而第二句的動詞可省去時：

My granddad keeps ferrets; my grandma poisonous snakes.
我的祖父飼養雪貂；祖母則養毒蛇。

冒號（The colon）：（：）

冒號（colon）常表示接下來的是例子、解釋或清單。可在下列情況使用：

- 介紹清單或例子時（如現例）
- 分開兩個陳述句子（statements），而第二句用作解釋第一句時：

Many workers were late this morning: the fog caused delays on the roads.
今早有很多工人遲到：霧氣延誤了交通。

- 介紹很長的引文（quotation）時
- 在劇本（plays）中標示説話

詞彙裏的標點符號 Punctuation within words

連字符號（Hyphens）：（ - ）

- 連結兩個或以上的詞彙，形成一個新的複合詞（compound word）：
  sun-tanned（曬黑的）、up-to-date（最新的）
- 分隔開前綴與詞根，以避免難看的字母組合：
  co-ordinate（協調）、pre-eminent（傑出的）
- 避免跟現存的詞彙混淆：
  re-cover（換上新的套子）
- 跟大楷字母合併時使用：
  U-turn（掉頭）、T-junction（丁字路口）

撇號（Apostrophes）：（ ' ）

- 標示省略的字母：
  can't = cannot（不能）
- 表示物主：
  the girl's pens（女孩的筆）≠ the girls' pens（女孩們的筆）

句號（Full stop）：（ . ）

句號常使用於表示詞彙縮寫：

a.m.（上午）、Feb.（二月）、etc.（等等）

句子中的標點符號 Punctuation within sentences

破折號 The dash：（ — ）

英語專家不常接受破折號（dash），但它很有用。破折號主要用在記錄英語口語，它可用於表示：

- 突然改主意：

  Let's talk about bananas — no, perhaps we'll cover pineapples first.
  來談談香蕉——不好，我們還是先說鳳梨。

- 插入句中強而有力和額外的意思（如那些不足以用逗號表示其力量的意思）
- 冗長的猶豫

省略號（The ellipsis）：（ ... ）

除了為句子作結之外，也可在句中使用三點以表示詞彙給刻意省略了。省略號（ellipses）通常用於重複引文時：

We will fight them on the beaches… we shall fight in the hills; we shall never surrender.
我們會在海灘上跟他們對戰……我們會在山上作戰；我們永不言敗。

括號（Brackets）：（ ）

括號（brackets）括着句中事後想起的詞彙或詞組，或解釋句中意思：

The referee (my Dad) made some unfortunate decisions. He sent me off (even though he knew Mum would be furious with hum when we got home).
那位球證（我的父親）下了錯誤的決定。他判罰我出場（即使他知道回家後媽媽會對他大法雷霆）。

說話中的標點符號 Punctuation of speech

引號（Quotation marks [' ' 或 " "]），又名倒轉的逗號（inverted commas）或說話符號（speech marks），用於書面上標示說話者確實的說話。這樣的說話稱為直接引語（direct speech）。若是用手寫出來的話，便用雙引號（double quotation marks [" "]）。

戲劇中的標點符號 Punctuations of plays

為了避免使用太多引號（speech marks），劇本（plays）有一套特定的標點符號（punctuation）使用方法：

1. 佈景（setting）及演員位置（position of actors）的描述以斜體字（italics）印製。（若是手寫稿，便用方括號 [ ] 括着。）
2. 角色（characters）名稱以大楷（capital letters）寫出。
3. 所有動作（movement）及聲音（voice）指示都寫在括號（brackets）內。
4. 除非角色人物引述直接引語（direct speech），否則切勿用引號（quotation marks）。

語言的特別運用 Special uses of language

標準英語 Standard English

標準英語（standard English）是「正式」英語（'official English'）的名稱 —— 遵守字典（dictionaries）和語法書（grammar books）規則的一套英語，亦即在商業書信（business letters）和正式文章中運用的英語，同時也是大部份電視新聞記者的用語。

非正式語言 Informal language

慣用語 Idioms

慣用語（Idioms）是在特定語言中具特別意義的短語（phrases），外地人常覺得這些慣用語難以理解或翻譯。'idiom' 一詞源自相同希臘詞根 'idiot'，意謂私人的、獨有的、只屬於一人的東西：

Use your loaf and get cracking!
動動腦筋，開始工作！

陳詞濫調 Clichés

陳詞濫調（cliché）是陳腐過時的用語，現已失去震撼力與新鮮感，但電視和電台仍不時使用。可嘗試找出它們，但切勿運用！例如：*first and foremost* 首要

俚語 Slang

俚語（slang）是日常生活中使用的詞彙和短語，但仍不為禮貌或正式對話所接受。俚語不會用於正式文章（除了記錄對話，或製造特別效果，如幽默感之外）。

特別效果 Special effects

頭韻 Alliteration

頭韻（alliteration）意謂重複使用開首字母（通常是輔音 [consonant]）或聲音以製造效果。這方法可使讀者更容易記着某短語。許多書名和廣告也用頭韻：

Charlie and the Chocolate Factory《查理與巧克力工廠》

對偶 Antithesis

對偶（antithesis）放兩個相反的主意在一個句子內，以帶出兩者之間的對比：

The wisest fool in Christendom (said about King James I).
世上所有基督教國家中最聰明的傻瓜（談論詹姆士王一世）。

半諧音 Assonance

半諧音（assonance）是兩個或以上的字母之間的元音（vowels）押韻（輔音 [consonants] 不押韻）。押韻詞彙的相隔距離必須足以製造效果：

Better than voices of winds that sing 比懂歌唱的風聲更美好

委婉語 Euphemism

委婉語（euphemism）是間接或刻意婉轉的方法，來指出一些令人不快的事情：

意思：death（死亡）

委婉語：passing away、passing on 或 falling asleep

非正式語言 Informal language

口語用語 Colloquialisms

口語用語（colloquial phrases）相等於俚語用語（slang expressions），為多數人所熟悉。除最正式的對話外，在所有對話中也得以運用。口語用語（colloquialism）同時也可以是慣用語（idiom）。

He gave the driver a dirty look.
他以厭惡的眼神看着司機。

術語 Jargon

術語（jargon）意謂在某商界（trade）、行業（profession）或排外的羣體（exclusive group）使用的特有詞彙和短語。對外界人來説，術語並不容易理解：

在滑浪的術語中，'wipe out' 解作倒下或傾覆。

比喻 Figures of speech

比喻（figure of speech）即任何非依照字面本義解釋的詞彙（word）或短語（phrase），又或是慣用語（idiom）。也就是説，這些詞彙或短語的意思並非字面上的意思。例如：'it's raining cats and dogs' 並不是説每當陰雲密佈時也要小心會有狗兒、貓兒從天上掉下來；'your bedroom is a pigsty' 也非説衣櫃裏會有小豬走出來。使用比喻的最常見方法有三種：

比喻語言 Figurative language　　　明喻 Simile
暗喻 Metaphor

特別效果 Special effects

影射 Innuendo

影射（innuendo）透過提示或暗示表達意思，通常是因為要説一些令人不快的話：

That new gold watch you are wearing is remarkably like the one I lost last month!
你戴着的新買金製手錶跟我在上一個月遺失的手錶非常相似！

反語 Irony

反語（irony）即説話跟意思相反（opposite），通常可從説話者的語氣清楚得知：

Teacher to dozy, inattentive class: 'You're a really bright lot this afternoon!'
教師對昏昏欲睡、毫不留心的學生説：「這個下午你們真是一羣聰明伶俐的人！」

擬聲詞 Onomatopoeia

擬聲詞（onomatopoeia）運用跟描述聲音相似的詞彙：

splash（撲通一聲的濺潑聲）

諺語 Proverb

諺語（proverb）是教導人生哲理的一些普及的簡短格言：

A stitch in time saves nine. 及時行動可為日後省掉額外工夫。

自己動手做溫習卡
Now, it is your turn to create your own revision cards

語法主題
Grammar Topic

1. 可能是個人覺得困難的英語語法範疇。
2. 可能是考試相關的內容，需要強化訓練。
3. 可能是易混淆的語法主題。

重點
Key Points

1. 參考本書，列出重點。
2. 不需要用完整句子寫出來，用關鍵詞或短語即可。
3. 最好每個重點配上一兩個例句，方便記憶。

我的筆記
My Notes

1. 提醒自己在該語法主題內不重複犯錯。
2. 記下自己的學習進度。
3. 提醒自己的學習目標。

* 便攜使用
可在左上角用釘孔機釘孔，用不同顏色的活頁圈代表不同語法主題，按照自我預計之進度，圈起合適數量和主題的溫習卡，以便在零碎時間如排隊、搭車時用溫習卡來溫習。

* 收納提示
1. 準備一些鞋盒，在盒面寫上語法主題，按主題存放溫習卡。
2. 準備家居常用的掛牆收納袋，用小衣夾夾住主題小卡，按主題存放溫習卡。

My Revision Card [01]

Grammar Topic
例如：你覺得困難的英語語法點是造詞。

Key Points
a) 例如：造反義詞，要先翻查該詞的本義。
b) 例如：造動詞，記住 -en, -fy 這些後綴可以造動詞。

My Notes
a) 例如：你設定三天內看完第一章造詞部份並完成練習。
b) 例如：不要混合暗喻一起使用。